Bittersweet Memories

An Oak Harbor Series

Kimberly Thomas

Prologue

Five months ago

"Oh thank God." Jules hurriedly pushed open the glass door of the restaurant and stepped inside. She peeled the coat from her body while resisting the urge to shake her head like a dog to get rid of the water dripping from her hair. The perfectly formed blond ringlets were completely gone, and her hair clumped to the sides of her head like a wet newspaper. If only she'd paid better attention to the icons the small Asian woman on the television had been pointing to during the weather news back at the apartment, she wouldn't have left without an umbrella. However, she was happy to be inside, where it was warm and dry while the rain continued to beat menacingly against the pavement, the roofs, and the awnings of the buildings.

After hanging her coat by the rack at the door, she kicked off her Chucks and placed them on the shoe rack. Spotting her friends at the far corner of the restaurant, she made a beeline for them.

"There she is. The woman of the hour," her best friend Katie greeted with a wide grin. All eyes were turned to her.

Jules gave her friends an apologetic smile as she sat on the floor and folded her legs. "I'm sorry I'm late."

"We were beginning to think you'd never show," Kylie, who was more Katie's friend than Jules's, said with what Jules could only describe as feigned concern.

"I got caught in the rain," she explained, averting her gaze to look at the various dishes lining the circumference of the table. It all looked very appetizing and smelled even better from the aromas hitting her nose. Her belly grumbled with need. But, just as quickly as the desire came to sample the food, it went with the feeling of wanting to vomit.

"You should try the Galbitang. It's really good," Stephen, another one of her friends, suggested, distracting her from her troublesome feelings.

"Okay, I'll go with that first, then," Jules agreed, accepting the bowl of beef soup he offered to her. She quickly took a few sips and mewled in satisfaction at the warmth filling her empty stomach as the rich, hearty soup made its way down her throat.

"I still can't believe we're almost done with our degrees," Samantha, the final person at their table, beamed.

"Yeah," Katie agreed. "Just think about it. Next February, we will be holders of bachelor's in international relations going on to do great things at the UN as ambassadors and making this world a better place," she finished in a diplomatic tone.

The group of friends looked at each other knowingly before bursting into laughter.

"We'd be lucky to fill the volunteer positions, let alone become ambassadors," Samantha chimed in with a shake of her head. The others nodded in agreement.

"Oh come on, guys. I know that we're more than capable of

doing exactly what we set out to do. There's no way we're going to allow anything to get in our way of achieving our goal," Jules countered. "Look at where we are now," she continued, arms wide open.

"A restaurant?" Katie asked, her brows scrunched up in confusion.

"No, silly. I was talking about the fact that we are here in Seoul because we believed we could study anywhere to be great. Even when they said there would be too much of a language barrier, we didn't listen. We came, and we conquered, and we loved it. For that reason, the future is definitely looking bright."

"Here, here—"

"Here."

Jules's group of friends all agreed in unison as they raised the small glasses of *yakju* to their lips and finished it off in one go.

"Cheers to an August of fun," Katie added while the others grinned and nodded in agreement.

Jules's smile turned into a grimace as the uneasy feeling resurfaced with a vengeance. She put her hand over her mouth as she hurriedly rose from the table and headed for the bathroom. The moment she entered the stall, she fell to the floor as the contents of the meal forcibly exited her mouth into the toilet bowl. She spent the next two minutes retching, waiting for the urge to vomit and the feeling of dizziness to subside. When she was sure that it was over, she slowly got to her feet and made her way to the sink to rinse her mouth. She took in her appearance in the mirror and cringed.

Her face looked pallid and clammy all at once, and her bedraggled hair made it even worse. Sighing tiredly, she turned on the tap and ran water into her cupped palms before splashing the cool liquid over her feverish skin. After a few more splashes, she patted her face dry with the hand towel from the dispenser. She proceeded to make her way back to the table.

"How are you feeling?" Katie asked the minute she sat down.

"I'm feeling much better. Thanks." Jules's lips turned up in a reassuring smile. Katie's green gaze burrowed into her before they furrowed in skepticism, but she didn't say anything further.

"I don't know, Jules. You obviously have something. This is the fourth time I've seen you with an upset stomach in the past week," Samantha noted before adding in a worried tone, "are you sure you didn't pick up a stomach bug?"

"That would explain it. I mean, Sam's right. You haven't been able to keep anything down for a while now." Katie gave her a pointed look. "It has to be that you've caught a stomach virus—"

"Or it could be that she's pregnant."

Every eye at the table turned to look at Kylie in shock.

"Kylie," Katie spoke forcefully.

"What?" she asked defensively. "You're all acting like Little Miss Perfect is too much of a Goody Two-shoes for that to happen to her. I don't think she has a bug, so the only other logical explanation is that she's pregnant," she argued.

The entire table was silent, including Jules, whose heart beat wildly against her chest as the feeling of bile and panic clambered its way up her throat.

"Jules is not pregnant. End of story," Katie broke the silence to affirm.

Stephen and Samantha bobbed their heads in agreement with Katie's statement, even though their own eyes shone with uncertainty.

"Now, can we please get back to finishing this very expensive meal and finish planning our vacation?"

The conversation picked up from where it had left off

before Jules had dashed off to the bathroom but try as she might, Jules could not keep up. Her mind was in turmoil, and it felt as if a fist had found its way around her heart, squeezing it so tight that the pain was unbearable. She didn't touch any of the food for the rest of the evening but drank the rose tea they'd ordered to help calm her stomach. Katie kept throwing worried glances in her direction while Kylie glowered at her whenever their eyes met.

Jules was glad when it was time to leave the restaurant and even happier when they stepped outside, and the evening sky that had transitioned into a deep purplish blue did not have a hint of moisture in it.

"Who's game for some late-night drinking and fun at Sub Zero? I heard they're having a live performance from one of the popular K-pop boy bands," Kylie suggested, looking hopefully around the group.

"I am definitely for it. I'm not ready for this night to end," Stephen readily agreed.

"Okay," Samantha also agreed.

"What do you say, Jules. Do you wanna go?" Katie turned to ask her best friend.

From the corner of her eye, she could see Kylie with her hands folded across her chest and her brows furrowed in a deep frown as she looked in their direction.

"No. That's fine. I think I'm just gonna go back to the apartment and get some rest."

"Want me to come with you to make sure you're all right? I can make my grandma's chicken soup."

"No. Go have fun. You deserve to instead of always taking care of me," Jules pushed. She could see Kylie shake her head in displeasure, and she didn't want there to be any more tension than there had already been between her and the girl. It was evident that Kylie, who Katie had met a few months ago in one of her elective classes, was trying to monopolize her time and freeze Jules out. Naturally, Jules would have fought to remind her who was Katie's best friend, but not tonight.

"You deserve this," she spoke earnestly.

Katie looked unsure and opened her mouth to say something, but Kylie beat her to it.

"Can we go now? Julia will manage without you for this one night, Kat. Let's go."

Katie's head turned to her group of friends waiting expectantly behind her before her green gaze fell on Jules once more with an apology.

"Go," Jules implored. "I'll see you when you get back."

With that, the four left in the opposite direction, and Jules watched them with a small upturn of her lips as they talked and laughed down the street. Turning around, she made her way down the sidewalk toward the bus stop.

Kylie's words from earlier popped into her head. Instinctively, her hand reached up to touch her tummy. She remembered that she'd been late for more than a month now. Initially, she'd thought it had been because she was so stressed about her finals, but now she wasn't so sure. Spotting the Korean sign for pharmacy on the corner of a building across the street from her, she quickly made her way over to it and stepped inside.

Jules walked up to the shelves that ran from one end of the room to the next, perusing the various items there. She could make out the names of some, mostly those in English, but the Korean ones proved formidable for her. Finally, she was able to identify what she'd come in to get. After grabbing a few boxes, she headed to the cashier with her head low. She kept her head down as she placed the items on the counter and waited for the old man to check them. She quickly dropped them into her handbag and rushed out of the store to her bus stop. She was just in time to see the bus pulling up, and she hurriedly got on, making her way to the back. For the whole ride, she could focus on nothing else other than the items that seemed to be burning a hole in her bag and what she had to do when she got home.

In less than twenty minutes, Jules was in her apartment. Removing her coat, she removed the boxes from her bag and made her way to the bathroom. After following the instructions, she sat on the toilet seat as she waited for the time to pass. As the seconds ticked by, the silence of the room became deafening. She tapped her leg in rapid succession, feeling as if she was going crazy. She jumped, frightened by the timer on her phone going off. She walked gingerly toward the sink and grabbed the first stick, bringing it to her face.

All the blood drained from her face when she saw the two pink lines in the result window. She quickly scooped up the others, desperate for them to contradict the first result, but they all displayed two pink lines. The sticks fell from her hand and landed in the sink with a clatter. Her legs felt like lead, so Jules returned to sitting on the toilet seat. She rested her head against her palms as her elbows rested on her legs for support. Her head felt as if it was about to explode.

How could this have happened?

A tear slipped down her cheek at the shame she felt. Slowly, she slid to the floor and brought her legs up to her chest as she buried her head between them, allowing the flood of tears to fall unhindered. She wasn't sure when the tears had subsided or when she had fallen asleep. She felt herself being shaken and her name being called.

"Jules. Wake up. What's wrong?"

Her eyes slowly opened to see her friend's face hovering over her in concern.

"What's wrong? Why are you sleeping in the bathroom?"

Jules gradually raised herself up to a sitting position and rested her back against the tub.

"Jules, you're scaring me. Your eyes are puffy, and you look very sick. Maybe we need to go to the emergency room. I'm gonna call Mike to come to pick us up."

"No. Don't do that. I'm not...sick," Jules managed to get through her lips.

Katie looked up from her phone to stare at her friend, with her brows turned up in concern. "Then what's wrong? I hate seeing you like this," she revealed.

Jules turned her head, not sure how to tell her friend.

"Jules, it's me. You know you can talk to me," Katie coaxed, coming to sit beside her, and taking her hand in hers.

Jules turned to her with tears in her eyes. "I'm...I'm pregnant."

Katie's green eyes widened in shock. "Are you sure," she asked after some seconds of silence.

"Check the bathroom sink," Jules advised her.

Katie got up and went to the sink, her hand covering her mouth at the evidence staring back at her.

"Oh no, Jules. I'm so sorry." Katie sighed, walking over to Jules and gathering her in her arms as she sobbed uncontrollably.

"Have you told Noah?" Katie asked Jules when her sobs slowed to soft whimpers.

"He's deployed, remember. I can't reach him because I have no idea where he is," Jules answered.

"What about the number for his parents?"

"What about it?" Jules asked, lifting her head from her friend's chest.

"He told you to call them in case of an emergency. I'm pretty sure this qualifies as an emergency," Katie reasoned.

At the look of hesitation on Jules's face, Katie pressed, "Call them." She rose and held her hand out to Jules, helping her to stand up. The two women exited the bathroom, and Jules went over to the couch to retrieve her cell phone before heading into her room to get the number.

Katie watched as she dialed the number and put the phone against her ear. The call was answered after the third ring.

"Hello?" A female who sounded too young to be Noah's mother answered the phone.

"H-hello is this the residence of the McKinleys?" she nervously asked.

"Yes, it is. How can I help you?" the woman asked.

"Um...well...I'm a friend of Noah's. I was hoping to talk with his mother or father," Jules replied.

There was a small pause on the line before the woman responded, "You can talk to me. I'm his fiancée, Dina."

Jules drew in a sharp breath, feeling as if the rug had just been pulled from beneath her.

"H-His...his fian- fiancée?" she stuttered.

Katie's eyes widened in surprise.

"That's right," the woman replied. "What is the message you wanted to leave?"

"Uh, um, never mind. I'll call back another time." Jules quickly ended the call and sagged against the couch, her world shattering into a million pieces.

Katie sat beside her and held her hand wordlessly in support. An hour later, Katie managed to get her to call her mom, and like before, she watched Jules dial the number and put the phone to her head.

After the third ring, her mother picked up.

"Hello?"

"Mom."

"Hi, sweetie. I'm so happy you called," Cora chirped.

Dread settled in her chest like a cannonball. "Mom...I need to tell you something."

"What is it, sweetie?" Cora asked, getting into protective mother mode.

"Mom. I'm pregnant."

There was a long pause after her revelation as she waited for her mother to say something.

"Mom...are you there?"

"I am, sweetie. This is what I need you to do..."

Jules listened attentively to what her mother instructed before disconnecting the call with a heavy sigh.

"What did she say?" Katie asked.

Jules looked up at her friend with sadness.

"I'm booking a flight back to the States. I'm heading to Oak Harbor."

Chapter One

Present Day

Jules reclined on the Adirondack with a thick blanket settled over her as she looked out at the snow-covered landscape from the side porch of her grandparents' home. The bare limbs of the trees bowed under the pressure of snowflakes that fell on them, hardening to glassy icicles as they clung to the branches and trunks of the trees. The shrubs along the sides of the house that retained their leaves were not exempted from the icy flakes that lay heavily on them, pushing their limbs toward the earth. The brilliance of the evening sun penetrated the thick gray clouds that blanketed the sky, casting its orange glow across the horizon as it fell on the dark-green waters of the harbor, creating a magnificent reflection of its splendor.

Jules absently rubbed her slightly swollen belly under the blanket; the friction of skin against the material generated heat that seeped through her sweater, warming her flesh. The fire crackled in the gas pit, sending out its heat for her to remain comfortable in the position she was in.

She continued to enjoy the scenery in front of her before her thoughts deviated, and she was forced to think about what led her to being in Oak Harbor. Five months ago, she'd been overcome with happiness that life was going better than she could have ever expected. She was in her final year of college; she had a boyfriend whom she was looking forward to building a deeper connection with when he got back from his tour, and she'd also had a job lined up once her degree was completed. All of that came to a screeching halt the moment she found out she was pregnant. She had been facing a plethora of challenges ever since. She'd decided to sit out her final semester. She erased all ties with the father of her child because he turned out to be a lying cheat, and ultimately, she'd had nothing but her thoughts to contend with over the past couple of months while everyone else continued to move forward and make progress. It was as if life had carried on without her while she stood still, watching and praying for it all to just be a bad dream.

What made it worse was that she didn't have anyone to talk to. She was surrounded by more family than she'd ever had around when growing up, and yet she felt completely alone. Her mother had tried to talk to her, tried to understand her, but each attempt had only resulted in her making matters worse, and it didn't help that every time she looked at Jules, all Jules could see was the disappointment swimming in her eyes. The one person she thought she could always count on being there for her became the most distant throughout her predicament. She thought she and Erin would have had time to talk about what had happened and that she could have helped her make the right decision, but Erin left immediately after her cousin Rory's wedding. She was disappointed that her own sister could treat her this way. They had always been each other's confidantes, and now it felt as if Jules knew nothing about what was going on in her sister's life, and Erin didn't seem at all bothered that she didn't know what was going on in Jules's life.

The ringing of her phone brought her out of her musings. She pulled the device from under the covers and opened it to see an incoming call from her best friend. Her heart leaped. She hadn't spoken to Katie in over three months. Drawing in a deep breath and releasing slowly, she pressed the answer button.

"Hello?" she answered tentatively.

"Hi, Jules," her friend answered in an equally cautious tone.

"Hi, Katie."

There was a brief pause as they both struggled with what to say.

"How are you?" Katie finally asked, breaking the crackling silence.

"I'm...okay," Jules breathed out, sitting up straighter on the chair. "And you?"

"I'm good."

There was another pause as the two women danced around the topic that had led to them not communicating.

Katie inhaled deeply before exhaling gradually. "Look, Jules. I'm sorry about what I said to you about throwing away your life and all that. It wasn't my place to say those things, and I know now that I need to respect your wishes and support you the best way I can as your friend," she rushed out in one breath. "I just want you to know that I'm really, really sorry, and I miss you."

Jules's beamed as her chest warmed over with emotion.

"I miss you too," she confessed. "And I'm sorry for shouting at you. You had every right to say what you did. I shouldn't have gotten so angry because I knew you were only looking out for my best interest."

"Classes haven't been the same without you."

A tear slipped down Jules's cheek. "I wish I was there," she revealed sadly.

"Hey, don't cry. I'm sorry I brought it up. Let's talk about something more...something more cheerful. Did I ever tell you what happened to my cat, Franny on the farm back home?"

"No," Jules said through her tears, already knowing that this was going to be a very funny story. Katie always had the funniest stories about the animals back on her family farm in Ohio, where she grew up. They always made Jules laugh, no matter how terrible her mood was.

As Katie launched into the story, Jules chortled uncontrollably about how much she enjoyed the story. By the time her friend was finished, she was holding her tummy as laughter shook her body, causing her to heave from the exertion of it all.

"Thank you," she breathed out appreciatively when she was able to catch her breath.

"Any time," Katie replied.

"Please, let's not wait this long to talk to each other again, and keep me updated on everything happening at school. I may not be there, but at least I can live vicariously through you," Jules implored.

"Will do," Katie said after a brief pause.

"Take care."

"Bye."

The smile remained glued to Jules's lips after she hung up with her friend, but her eyes also glistened with unshed tears. The call had been pleasant, but it was also a reminder that she'd given up so much, and though she tried to keep her emotions in check, it was impossible when she was alone with her thoughts. A tear glided down her face and then another until they started running into each other in their mad dash to hang precariously off her chin before landing against the blanket. It was glaringly obvious to her that she was a failure.

As the tears dwindled, Jules released a gust of air, and she sagged against the chair once more, resting the phone beside her. She felt tiny flutters in her belly before a tiny jab landed against her navel. Automatically, her hand rested against her stomach, and she grinned to herself as another jab pulsed against her palm.

"Hi, sweetie," she cooed, rubbing her belly soothingly. "I know it might feel confusing now, but I just want you to know how much I love you already. I can't wait to meet you." She continued to run her hands over her belly as she stared out at the sky, transitioning through a spectrum of orange, pink, and blue hues as the sun descended over the horizon. "No matter what happens, I will always love you, and I will make sure you're protected," she absolved.

"Hi."

Jules's head flung upward until her eyes connected with her mother's blue-gray ones staring down at her.

"Hi," she returned softly.

"I thought you might want something warm. It's really cold out here, even with the fire going and all," Cora expressed, handing her daughter one of the steaming mugs she held before taking a seat on one of the chairs beside her.

Jules brought the cup up to her lips and sipped the hot beverage, welcoming the warmth as it traveled down her throat to settle in her chest.

"Thanks for the hot chocolate," she said, raising the cup in gratefulness.

"You're welcome," Cora replied, beaming. She took a few sips from her own cup and turned to look out at the activities of nature.

The two sat in silence for some time before Cora finally spoke.

"Have you heard from your sister?" she asked.

"No, I haven't," Jules replied, fixing the blanket more firmly around her frame.

Cora's head moved up and down in understanding as her eyes glassed over and her lips pursed in concern. "I've been trying to get a hold of her since she left, but her phone keeps going to voicemail," she revealed.

"I'm sure she's fine," Jules spoke dismissively and turned to look straight ahead of her.

Cora turned to her daughter, a look of surprise on her face. Slowly, her head returned to its original position.

Silence ensued for some time again until Cora chose to speak up.

"Jules, I don't know when we stopped talking or how the trust we used to share became so broken, but I wish I could have prevented that because I can see that you have so much bottled up inside and that it's taking a toll on you. I want to help you, but I don't even know how or where to start."

Jules didn't know how to respond to her mother's words. She did miss them being able to talk about any and everything, but ever since her dad cheated on her mom, she'd started telling her less and less about what was happening in her life. She hadn't even told her that she had been in a relationship which had probably made her pregnancy news all the more shocking. At the time, she'd rationalized that Cora was going through so much with the divorce, then her dad dying, and her having to move to Oak Harbor to take care of Grandma Becky.

She hadn't wanted to add to all that. But then she'd found out she was pregnant and had no one else to call but her mother. She'd heard the disappointment in Cora's voice when she'd instructed her to come home. It hit even more forcefully when Cora wouldn't look at her when she picked her up at the port in Clinton. Whenever their eyes would accidentally meet, Jules could see the dissatisfaction in their blue-gray depths.

That's when she started feeling even more alone, as if what happened to her had been the most unforgivable thing.

"I want you to know that I love you very much. You and your sister are my greatest pride and joy, and no matter what, that will never change. I just don't..." Cora released an unsure breath. "I only want what's best for you...and for the baby."

Jules wanted to refute her mother's claims, but still, she remained silent.

"Whatever you decide to do, just know that I am here for you, and I will stand by your decision."

She looked over at her mother with a slight lift of her lips in acknowledgment.

"Thanks," she replied simply before returning her attention to the covered landscape where everything was hidden under the perfectly laid snow. She brought the warm beverage to her lips and took a few more sips.

The sky was almost completely dark at this time, and the porch lights came on automatically, filling and brightening the space.

"I'm gonna go check on Mom," Cora informed her, rising from the chair she sat on. "Remember to put out the fire when you're coming in."

"Okay," Jules replied plainly, not bothering to look at her mother. Cora made her way inside.

As she pondered what her mother had said, Jules realized she didn't even know what was best for herself let alone what was best for the baby that was getting bigger with each passing moment. All she knew was that she loved her baby more and more every day, but she also didn't know if she had what it took to be the best mother for her.

It scared her to death.

Chapter Two

Eleven months ago

"Tale as old as time."
"Song as old as rhyme."
"Beauty and the beast. Oh, oh, oh-oh...Beauty and the beast."

Jules held on to Katie as they belted out the last set of lyrics that appeared on the screen. At the end of their duet, they turned to see their friends staring at them, awestruck.

"Oh my gosh. You guys...you're amazing," Samantha, who was the first one to recover, praised. She brought her hands up and applauded. Soon the others joined in, cheering and complimenting how well they sounded together— all but one.

Jules and Katie giggled, deliriously happy with their friends' reactions. After bowing, they took their seats.

"All right, who's next?" Steven asked.

"I'll go," Kylie volunteered. She gingerly made her way to

the raised platform and keyed in the song she wanted on the karaoke machine. The lyrics of the song immediately popped up on the monitor as the first few chords of an upbeat number permeated the small room they'd rented for this. When Kylie belted out the first few notes, the group cheered loudly, rocking along in support.

"Aren't you glad you decided to come tonight?" Katie all but shouted into Jules's ear.

Jules smiled broadly while nodding and giving her friend the thumbs-up.

Katie nodded back approvingly before turning back to the brunette on the stage. When Kylie was finished, the group of friends allowed Stephen to fill their shot glasses with soju.

"Here's to another semester completed successfully and hopefully no failures," Allen, another of their friends, toasted.

They all raised their glasses in agreement before tilting their heads back and downing the content.

Jules was indeed happy. This meant that she only had a year left at Seoul University. She couldn't wait too finally be over it.

After a few more okay performances and some laughable ones, the group gathered their belongings and left the Noraebang.

Jules giggled as she stepped through the glass door onto the sidewalk. She felt herself hit what felt like a brick walk before she lost her balance and started falling. With eyes closed, she braced for impact with the concrete, but it never came. Hands that felt like bands of steel wrapped around her upper arms and pulled her swiftly upward.

"Are you all right?" a deep masculine voice asked the moment she was righted on her feet.

Jules looked up to see a tall guy looming over her. His eyes which she guessed were green, stared down at her with concern. She felt her pulse quicken at how good he looked. He wore a white shirt that stretched across his broad shoulders as it accentuated his lean physique. A pair of black joggers and black loafers completed his ensemble.

"I am fine, thanks," she managed to say, her heart fluttering wildly as his masculine scent mingled with the cologne he wore, assuaged her senses. Jules took a step back, and the guy's hands immediately fell from her arms. "I'm sorry for bumping into you like that," she apologized, pulling her coat tightly against her to ward off the icy cold air whistling around them.

"It's fine." The guy smirked, raking his fingers through his dirty blond hair and pushing back the strands that fell over his forehead. "I'm going to go. Your friends seem to be losing patience as well," he said, his eyes looking past her.

Jules turned to see her friends staring curiously back at them. "Right." She took another step back. "Again. Sorry about earlier. Bye." With that, she turned and walked over to her group of friends.

Katie gave her a knowing look that she chose to ignore. When she looked back, he was already gone.

"I don't want this night to end," Stephen chirped. "Let's go to that new club they opened."

And just like that, they'd ended up at the newly opened club, dancing wildly to a number of K-pop songs blaring from the speakers. Jules flailed her arms in the air and moved her body from side to side. Her eyes fluttered shut as she allowed the beat to move her. She felt herself bump into someone from behind, and she turned around to apologize, but her words caught in her throat at the person standing before her.

"We should stop meeting like this, or someone could get badly hurt," he joked, his voice raised above the noise to make sure she heard him.

Jules smiled sheepishly and turned to leave. Her eyes widened in surprise when she felt his hand wrap around hers. "Can I ask you for a dance?"

She hesitated for a bit before shaking her head yes. The

music changed to something softer, and Jules allowed him to bring her in closer with his hands on her waist. She reached up to wrap her hands around his neck and stared into his glittering eyes as they swayed to the music.

"I'm Noah, by the way," the handsome stranger introduced himself.

"I'm Julia, but everyone calls me Jules," she returned.

Noah bobbed his head slowly. "I like it," he replied, a toothy grin brightening his face.

For the second time that night, Jules felt her pulse quicken, and she quickly averted her eyes as she felt the heat creeping up her neck.

After the end of the song, Jules allowed him to walk her back to her seat, and Jules introduced him to her group of friends.

"Why don't you sit with us?" Katie suggested, ignoring the death glare Jules was giving her.

"I'm actually here with a bunch of my buddies," Noah explained.

"They can join us if they want," Samantha jumped in with an eager smile on her lips.

Jules groaned internally.

"All right, I'll go ask them."

In less than two minutes, Noah and three other guys who looked as if they lived in the gym joined Jules and her friends.

For the remainder of the night, Jules realized that while Noah's friends kept up the conversation with her friends, Noah seemed only interested in talking to her. Kylie, on numerous occasions, tried to get his attention but was unsuccessful, which Jules noticed left her sullen, and on more than one occasion, she caught the girl glowering at her.

At the end of the night, Jules was beat but satisfied with her decision to go out with her friends. March was less than a week away, which meant the beginning of her final year at college and one that she couldn't afford to entertain any type of distraction.

"Can I walk you and your friends to the bus stop?" Noah asked as they filed out of the club.

"Um...sure," she nervously agreed. "It's just Katie and me, though. The others live on campus," she explained.

After saying goodbye to their friends, Jules, Katie, Noah, and Bill, one of the guys from his group, turned and walked toward the bus stop. Jules noticed that Katie and Bill chose to walk ahead of them, which gave her the idea they were trying to play matchmakers.

"Our friends really aren't that subtle." Noah laughed beside her as he, too, picked up on what they were doing.

"No, they are not," Jules returned with a light chuckle of her own.

"Tonight was...different than what I had anticipated when the guys pushed me to come out with them," he continued to say. "I'm glad I did because I got to meet you," he finished, glancing over at her, his lips curled upward.

Her face broke out into a smile of its own as heat settled in her cheeks.

By the time they'd gotten to the bus station, Jules had exchanged numbers with Noah, and when they boarded the bus home, she couldn't help the grin that stretched across her face as she turned to see him watching the bus with hands in his pocket.

"Didn't I tell you that tonight would be an unforgettable one? I'm literally psychic," Katie professed with a self-satisfied smirk. She threw herself on the sofa in the small living room area they shared.

"Slow down there, Miss Cleo." Jules giggled, removing her coat and winter hat and hanging them on the hooks of the organizer by the door.

"I bet he'll be calling you any minute now," she said.

Jules's phone rang just then, and she quickly fished it out of her purse. Her lips automatically lifted, and Katie waved her fist triumphantly.

"Hello?"

"Hi. It's Noah...um...I was just calling to make sure that you made it home safely."

Jules's smile grew at the obvious nervousness in his voice. It was cute.

"I did. Thanks for checking."

There was a short pause on the line, and Jules looked up to see her friend silently ask her what she said.

Jules discreetly pressed the speaker.

"So, I know we just met—"

"You mean just bumped into each other," she countered.

"Yeah, that." He chuckled.

Noah's voice filled the small space and had Katie perched on the edge of the seat as she waited tentatively for him to continue. Jules wanted to laugh at how invested her friend was in this.

"I'm really glad we did because I've never met anyone quite like you, and I would like to get to know you better. Would you like to go on a date with me tomorrow? That's if you're free..."

Katie mouthed yes, her eyes urging her to do what her lips said.

"Okay. Yes."

* * *

Five months later

Jules held on to Noah as tightly as she could, her face buried in his chest, her tears staining his army T-shirt.

"It's gonna be all right, I promise. Eight months will run off so quickly, and it'll be like I never left." Noah ran his hand over her hair as he kept her face to his chest, the other hand rubbing her back soothingly. "I'll write often so that you'll know that I'm okay."

"Promise?" Jules raised her head to look into his forest green eyes that stared back at her lovingly.

"Promise," he affirmed. "There'll be some delay because the letters will have to go to the US before they get to you, but I promise I'll write often, and if you have any emergency and you need to reach me, just call the number I gave you for my folks."

"Why can't we have video calls like all the other couples I see in the movies?" she asked softly.

Noah chuckled. "We could, but I will be on special assignment, so no traceable forms of communication unless it's through the commanding officer," he explained.

Jules pouted.

"I wish you didn't have to go," she revealed with a crack in her voice.

"Me too," Noah replied, a little bit of sadness marring her face.

Leaning down, he planted a kiss against her lips. "I lo..."

Her heart skipped a beat as her breath caught in her throat.

Noah drew in a deep breath and released it before planting a grin on his lips. "I look forward to reading your letters."

Jules nodded in response as she processed her feelings toward his near confession. She wasn't sure if she was relieved or disappointed. He hadn't said it.

"I'll see you when you get back," she said, finally stepping out of his embrace.

Noah's green eyes searched her face before a smile graced his own lips.

"I'll see you when I get back," he returned, hauling himself into the back of the pickup that came to take him and his team to the base for deployment.

The vehicle pulled away, and Noah waved at her as it moved down the street until it disappeared from sight.

She felt as if there was so much that had been left unsaid

that day, but in the end, it didn't matter because Noah had proved himself to be a snake.

"I am his fiancée."

Jules woke with a start, her head pounding furiously. She wasn't sure why her mind kept bringing her back to Noah's duplicitous actions, but every time it caused her heart to pain as his deception had just happened yesterday. The baby stirring in her belly proved otherwise. Fresh tears rolled down her cheeks as she pulled herself up in the bed. Wiping angrily at the tears staining her cheeks, she flung her legs over the edge of the bed and made her way into the bathroom to find some painkillers in the medicine cabinet.

As far as she was concerned, Noah didn't deserve to be part of her baby's life for what he did.

Chapter Three

Jules threw on a sweater over her nightgown and slipped her feet into the fuzzy bed slippers before she padded across the room. She was surprised by the coldness that greeted her outside her bedroom. She hugged herself as a slight shiver passed through her. She turned to go to the den but paused as she looked across the hallway at her grandmother's door.

Jules walked over to the door, and just as she placed her hand on the knob, a sudden crash from inside the room caught her attention. Quickly, she pushed the door open.

"Grandma, are you—" The words stuck in her throat at the sight of Becky haphazardly hanging off the bed, her face buried in the quilt that covered the medical bed, her hands gripping the fabric as tightly as she could manage. Jules figured the wheelchair banging into the metal cabinet close to the door must have been what she heard.

Springing into action, she collected the wheelchair and brought it over to the bed.

"Here, let me help you," she offered, positioning the wheel-

Bittersweet Memories

chair, her hands rounding Becky's waist to help support her weight.

"N-N-Nooo...the b-b-baaab-y." Becky managed to lift her head to voice her own concern.

"It's fine, Grandma," Jules assured her. "The baby is fine."

Becky's grip on the quilt loosened, giving Jules the opportunity to help lower her into the waiting chair. She stepped back when Becky was secured to the chair.

"It's the middle of the night, Grandma. Where were you going?" Jules asked the woman whose eyes hadn't met hers yet.

"I w-wa-wanted t-to g-g-get some...thing to dr-drink," she replied softly.

"Why didn't you use the buzzer? You know Mom or one of the others would have come to get it for you," Jules reasoned.

Becky shook her head. "No."

Jules took the time to examine Becky. Her weight had reduced significantly over the past couple of months, leaving her looking like the pages of a very old book that would crumble at the slightest of touches. Her brown hair lay flat against her head, and her eyes, though still turned from Jules, she could see dark, purple bags under them. Jules felt as if her heart would crumble at how fragile the woman looked.

"Wh-why are y-you up?" Becky asked, surprising her.

"Um...I couldn't sleep," Jules replied, rubbing her wool-clad arm. "I was gonna get some hot chocolate and go to the den for a while," she finished.

"I...I'll j-j-join y-you," Becky said, finally looking up at her, expressing tenderness.

"Okay," Jules agreed, helping the woman out of the room and getting her to the den.

After getting them both some hot chocolate, Jules rekindled the wood in the hearth of the fireplace and settled beside her grandmother to watch reruns of *I Love Lucy*, Becky's favorite sitcom. The two laughed at the perfectly timed jokes from the characters. After some time, Jules's mind returned to her predicament. She felt the light grip from Becky's hand and looked over at her.

"What's wrong?" her grandmother asked clearly, her green eyes filled with concern.

Jules sighed, and her shoulders sagged as she looked away from her grandmother. After a long pause, she spoke.

"I don't...I can't..." Another heavy breath left her lips.

"I'm scared to have the baby," she turned to confess. "The baby is coming, and my life is out of control. I don't know what to do." Her gaze cast down to her lap.

"Br-bringing a n-new l-life in-to th-this world is sc-scary b-but it i-is th-the purest love y-you will ever f-feel when y-you f-f-first get to hold them and re-realize that y-you made this t-tiny l-little person. The f-feeling of b-being scared won't ever leave even when th-they be-become adults, b-but your love is what will h-help y-you to do what i-is righ-t for them."

Jules smiled, grateful for her grandmother's input.

"Just t-take it one st-step at a t-time b-but importantly w-work on wh-what needs fixing n-now...like t-telling th-the father ab-about your preg-nancy."

Jules's head pulled back as her eyes widened in surprise.

"How did you..."

"I just do," Becky finished her sentence with a knowing smile.

Jules's lips curled downward with regret. "Even if I wanted to tell him, I have no way of getting in contact with him. He's in the army and currently away from base camp. Communication is restricted. The last time I spoke with him was back in Seoul before he was deployed," she explained.

Becky's green eyes stared seriously back at her. "If-f you want-t-t him to know, you-u will-l-l find a way-y-y," she spoke intuitively.

Jules averted her eyes to stare at the characters moving

across the screen as she pondered her grandmother's words. It was true that if she wanted him to know, she had the means to get the information to him, but she wasn't sure she wanted him to know, not when her news had the potential to destroy so many lives. Her mind flashed to his fiancée he had back in South Carolina. Noah had betrayed her trust.

She heard an unusual crackling sound coming from Becky and the hand holding hers stiffening. Her head swung around, and she released an alarming gasp.

"Grandma, what's wrong?" she asked, jumping to her feet.

Instead of responding, Becky wheezed in succession as the veins in her neck worked profusely to swallow.

Not knowing what to do, Jules panicked.

"Mom, Aunt Andrea, Aunt Jo, come quick. It's Grandma!" she called frantically from the foot of the stairs.

In a few seconds, hurried footfalls sounded on the stairs before her mother and her aunts stood before her, faces filled with alarm and dread.

"What's wrong?" Cora managed to ask.

"Grandma...she looks like she's having a seizure," Jules answered.

They all rushed past her to find Becky in the den.

When her feet finally decided to cooperate, and she made her way back to the den, Aunt Jo was on the phone with the hospital while her mother and Aunt Andrea tried to unfurl her fists and her legs that had curled inward.

In less than ten minutes, an ambulance was at the door, and a couple of minutes later, Becky was being lifted into the ambulance. Cora climbed in after her, and her aunts took one of the cars to follow.

Jules watched helplessly as the sirens wailed as the ambulance took off down the path with her aunts traveling close behind it.

* * *

Cora paced the small space that was the waiting room of the hospital as she waited anxiously for news about her mother. It was all she could do to quiet the turmoil that was broiling her insides. She prayed fervently that this wouldn't be the day that she lost her mother. She looked over at her sisters, who sported similar expressions as they clung to each other, and she knew they were probably praying the same as she.

"Please, God. She needs more time...we need more time," she pleaded wordlessly.

All three heads immediately turned to the door at the sound of the knob turning. Tessa stepped through the door with her face drawn in concern.

"Hi. I just got in for my shift, and I heard the news. How are you guys holding up?" she asked as she stepped into the room and closed the door.

"Hey, Tess," Cora replied, accepting her cousin's hug. "They haven't told us anything yet, but we're trying to remain positive."

"Okay. If we don't get anything in the next fifteen minutes, I'll try to get some more information," Tessa assured her, hugging Andrea and Jo next.

"Thanks for being here, Tess," Andrea beamed.

"Of course. I don't think I would be able to get anything done until I know what's going on." Just then, her phone rang, and she removed it from her pocket. "It's Dad," she informed them after glancing at the screen. "Hi, Dad," she greeted. "Yeah, I'm here with them."

Tess held out the phone to Cora. "He wants to talk to you."

"Hi, Uncle Luke," Cora said the moment she put the phone against her ear.

"How're you holding up, kiddo?" he asked.

"Honestly..." Cora released a heavy breath and looked

around the room at the weary faces watching her. Excusing herself, she stepped into the corridor of the long hallway.

"I'm scared, Uncle Luke," she confessed as a tear finally slipped down her cheek. "I'm so sc-scared," her voice cracked as more tears began to fall.

After a short pause, Uncle Luke released a long breath. "I know, kiddo. I know. It's rough and even more so because you're the oldest who has to be strong for your sisters and for Becky."

"I don't know how to do that," Cora tearfully admitted.

"You do, Cora," Luke encouraged. "You've always been strong...the one that your sisters tried to emulate. You were the one that your father wasn't too worried about because you were his resilient girl— his *Silver Bullet*."

At the mention of her father, more tears pooled in her eyes before falling down her cheeks. Cora reached up to swipe at them.

"He was a man full of pride, and even though he didn't express it, he was proud of you, Cora. That's the reason he put you in charge of taking care of your mother and, by extension, without you realizing it, taking care of your sisters. He knew you had it in you to boost their morale."

"Thanks, Uncle Luke," Cora said, smiling through her tears.

"Anytime, kiddo," he replied simply. "Besides, Becky isn't going anywhere today. It's not her time— not until she is fully at peace."

The smile on Cora's lips widened at her uncle's words. From the corner of her eyes, she saw a flash of white, and she turned her head to see the doctor coming toward her.

"Uncle, I'll call you later. The doctor's here."

"Okay, kiddo. Bye."

"Bye."

"How is she, Doc?" were the first words out of her mouth as soon as the woman was standing before her.

The woman gave her a half smile. "Why don't we talk in the room with the rest of your family?" the woman suggested.

Cora's heart fell.

"All right," she agreed, opening the door and walking through it with the woman. As soon as her sisters saw them, they rose to their feet with anxious looks.

"Hi, ladies...Tessa," the doctor greeted.

"Sofia," Tessa greeted back while the others inclined their heads.

"I know it's been a rough couple of months for you all, and I wish I had better news to share, but the truth is...Becky's ALS has progressed to stage three."

There wasn't a sound in the room as all eyes remained riveted on her after she dropped the bomb.

The woman continued. "Becky is now completely paralyzed. That means she won't be able to carry out any of her bodily functions by herself. On top of that..." the woman paused before her eyes connected with Cora's, filling with remorse. "Becky also suffered a stroke that affected the left side of her body even more. It is more noticeable on her face. She will have to have a feeding tube because chewing and swallowing will be very difficult for her. Her lungs are deteriorating as well. It is advisable that you find a hospice for her or get an around-the-clock nurse to tend to her needs." The woman gave the family an apologetic look as she waited for them to process the information.

"How...how long does she have left?" Cora asked, already dreading the answer.

"Maybe six months tops, but...based on how quickly she is deteriorating, it might be as little as three months."

Cora felt as if a lump was lodged in her throat, cutting off her air supply and her feet felt like lead. Slowly, she backed up until she was leaning against the wall.

"Can they see her?" Tessa asked the question that none of the sisters were able to voice.

"They can." The woman inclined her head. When the doctor left, the sisters broke down in tears as they rushed to embrace each other. Tessa held them while trying to console them. When they separated, Tessa led the way to Becky's room.

After a short, hesitant breath, Cora turned the knob and pushed the door open, entering with her sisters. Slowly, they walked over to the bed where Becky was hooked up to tubes as the machine showing her vitals beeped steadily.

When they were all standing by the bed, Cora's heart slammed against her chest as her sisters released audible gasps of shock.

Even though the oxygen mask was covering her face, the sisters could see that the left side hung lower than her right.

Chapter Four

New Year's Eve

Laughter filled the Hamiltons' living room as the family came together to celebrate New Year's, which was only a few hours away. Although Christmas was over, the decorated tree still stood prominently in the corner of the room while the yuletide-themed stockings hung from the mantel, and the frosted green garlands and faux candles decorated the surface. The only addition to the decor was the gold "Happy New Year's" banner attached to the wall above the love seat.

It had always been a tradition for the entire family to celebrate all the holidays together, and ever since Sam's death and Becky's illness, it had become even more imperative that they made every moment together memorable.

"All right, everyone. Here's to another year filled with happiness and togetherness," Uncle Luke announced, raising his glass as an act of declaring the celebrations had officially begun.

Everyone raised their own glasses in agreement, and a small cheer went out throughout the room. When the noise subsided, Uncle Luke continued.

"We have lost so much, but in the process, we have also gained a lot. As we all know, Becky doesn't have much time left..."

The air in the room shifted, becoming thick with tension at the mention of Becky's condition.

"But, while we still have her here with us, we want to make the most of our time. With that being said, when it's time for the countdown, Cora, Drea, and Jo agreed with me that we should gather in her room and celebrate it with her. She's resting now, but hopefully, by the time we get to the countdown, she'll be well rested."

"That's a great idea," Kerry jumped in to say. The others murmured their agreement or nodded. "Here's to Aunt Becky for remaining so strong and resilient despite what's happening to her."

"To Becky."

"To Aunt Becky."

"To Mom."

Just like that, the atmosphere became lighter once more. Everyone went back to doing what they had been doing before Uncle Luke's speech.

Jules watched from the sofa beside the tree as her family talked and laughed, some drinking the spiced eggnog drink Kerry made while others sipped alcoholic beverages. She stared into her glass of cranberry juice. Her eyes clouded over, and her lips spread into a grim line. At that moment, all she could think of was how much life sucked.

Here she had an unplanned child with a man who turned out to be a lying cheat, her career was all but over before it even had the opportunity to take off, and her grandmother, who had the sweetest soul, was battling an incurable disease and literally on her death bed, yet still, everyone around her was cackling and having fun as if everything was okay.

Jules felt as if she was one step away from having a nervous breakdown. She wished she had someone to talk to about her feelings. Her mind switched to Erin, and a wave of uncharacteristic anger welled up in her chest. It hurt so much that in her time of need, Erin had all but disappeared. She wondered what she'd done to deserve being treated like a leper by her sister. The hurt fuelled her anger.

"All right, no more alcohol for you, young lady." Jules's gaze landed on Sharon just as she removed the glass of brown liquid from her daughter's grip and replaced it with a bottle of water.

"Mom, that's my first and only drink," Cassidy whined.

"Your mother's right, Cass," Bruce said sternly, coming to stand by his wife's side.

Cassidy looked back and forth between her parents, her eyes flashing with anger and her hands folded in on each other. Her lips trembled as she fought the urge to retort. Cassidy released a frustrated sigh and pushed away from the sofa she had been leaning on. She opened the water bottle on her way outside of the room.

Sharon released a heavy breath as her hand came up to rest against her chest. Her gaze remained fixed on the door her daughter had just exited. Her lips turned down. Charles rubbed his wife's back soothingly before steering her to the other side of the room.

Jules wondered why her cousin's parents cut off her alcohol consumption.

A surge of annoyance rose in her as she reflected on how easy it was for parents to treat their adult children like children and feel validated for doing so. Her thoughts switched to her father.

"I didn't tell you because I was trying to protect you."

"Protect me from what? From the fact that you're the reason our family is broken?"

"Jules, none of what I did was meant to hurt you."

Jules laughed sarcastically. "Yeah, well, it's a little too late for that now, isn't it?"

She shook herself out of the memory. She still hadn't come to grips with the fact that the man who could never do any wrong could have caused her the most hurt. He had torn apart their family with his cheating and deceit. She was pretty sure that everything that was happening now was a result of him. If she never saw him or heard from him ever again, she would be happy. Still, she couldn't deny that they'd been happy before. She remembered all the Christmases, all the birthdays, the New Year's celebrations they'd had together as a family. *What could have shifted to cause him to not be happy with what he already had?* Two years later and she still hadn't gotten the answer.

Jules searched the room until her gaze landed on Cora, who was standing by the door with Jamie. She was giggling at whatever he'd just said, her hand flattening against his chest as her head dipped low. A wide grin appeared on Jamie's lips as he pointed to the mistletoe above their heads.

Cora looked bashful before raising herself onto her toes to plant a kiss on Jamie's welcoming lips. Jamie's hands came around her back to hold her to him as he prolonged the kiss.

Jules's pulse quickened, and her chest tightened as her eyes narrowed at the two people across the room.

Cora looked over at her before turning to say something to Jamie, and he nodded. The two made their way in her direction.

"Hi, sweetie. How are you feeling?" Cora asked, the smile from before still plastered on her lips.

"I'm fine," Jules replied in a clipped tone.

Cora's blue-gray eyes widened in surprise, but her happiness was still apparent.

"Are you sure? I could go get something for you to eat..."

"I said I'm fine." Realizing her tone had been snappish, she said, "No thanks, Mom. I'm fine."

Cora opened her mouth as if to say something but slowly closed it, a confused look on her face.

"Jules, I'm really happy we could get to spend this time together," Jamie injected, trying to diffuse the tension.

Jules turned to the man beside her mother, a saccharine smile gracing her lips as she responded, "Well...at least one of us is happy and enjoying you taking the space that once belonged to my father." Her grin dropped, and her lips formed a thin line across her face.

"Jules," her mother gasped.

Before her mother could say anything else, Jules rose from her seat and walked out of the room. Even though the time was very cold, she found herself outside on the porch in need of some fresh air.

As she took in a huge gulp of the frigid air, it felt as if her lungs were on fire. She didn't feel that much relief from releasing her breath, but she took in shorter breaths at intervals to relieve the pressure on her lungs and chest.

A wave of guilt passed through her as her mind rolled back to how mean she had been to Jamie. He hadn't deserved those harsh words, but at the moment, all she had seen was red. *How dare her mother look happier with him than she'd ever been with her father? How could her smile be so wide and open? How could she be so free when Jules's life was crumbling before her eyes?*

She sighed, feeling dejected. Jamie truly hadn't deserved her ire, though. He had been nothing but good to her mother, and from what she'd already witnessed, he was a much better person than her father at this point. He seemed so attuned to her feelings, and it was as if his purpose in life was to make sure that Cora kept a smile on her lips. Joel had never been like that. In all the years she'd observed her parents' relationship, she hadn't realized that their happiness exceeded for their children and not for each other. Jules had been so busy that nothing else had mattered. Had she really been that blind all along?

At the sound of footsteps approaching, Jules glanced over her shoulder to see her mother. She turned back to look out at the snow and the trees illuminated by the full moon against the dark backdrop.

Cora came to stand beside her daughter. She didn't say anything for a full two minutes. She just stood there staring at the moon blessing them with her full, glorious luster.

"I won't pretend to know what is happening inside that head of yours, and I do understand that you're going through some things, but what you did in there was not only uncalled for, but it was also completely disrespectful and downright mean," Cora said, her voice flat.

"I'm sorry. I don't know what came over me," Jules responded, glancing over at her mother before looking back out at the unmoving figures.

Her mother gazed at her helplessly for a minute. "The person you need to apologize to is inside," she said sternly. "I hope you will do the right thing." With that, Cora returned to the party.

Jules sighed defeatedly. After a few more minutes, she walked back inside with her head bowed in remorse and shame. Spotting Jamie and her mother talking to her aunt Andrea and her boyfriend, she slowly made her way over to them.

Cora was the first to notice her. She gave her a subtle nod, and her lips slightly curled upward in encouragement.

"Um, excuse me, Jamie. Can I talk to you, please?"

Jamie turned to her, a grin on his lips. "Sure," he replied easily.

Jules felt her heart rate quicken and her palms become sweaty as she walked over to a quiet area to render her apology.

"I'm really sorry about the way I spoke to you earlier. If I could take it back, believe me, I would."

Jamie gave her an understanding look. "It's okay. I know it can be hard to accept someone new coming into your life, especially if you see that as taking over a role that once belonged to your father. I want you to know that I have no intention of trying to be your father. I'm not trying to replace him, but I would like to be your friend if you'll allow me."

Jules felt the guilt from earlier. How could she be mean to such a cool person?

"I would like that," she said.

"Great." He turned to leave.

"Jamie..."

Jamie twisted around to look at Jules.

"Please take care of her," she spoke in earnest.

Jamie's eyes became serious. "With all my heart," he replied.

Jules gave him a grateful smile that remained on her lips as he made his way to her mother.

Cora looked over at her daughter, beaming.

Jules felt her lips widen even further in response.

Chapter Five

"All right, everyone. We're five minutes away from the new year. I think it's time we start making our way to Becky's room," Uncle Luke informed everyone.

In less than a minute, the whole family was crammed into Becky's bedroom. Becky was propped up with pillows behind her back. A feeding tube ran from her nose, and an oxygen mask rested around her neck. Jules made her way over to her grandmother, reaching down to unfold her frail and paralyzed hand in hers. Becky's lips curved into a grin that transformed the right side of her face while the left side remained unmoved.

She mustered the brightest smile she could manage as her grandmother stared back at her, her eyes saying more than words could ever convey.

"I know everything will be okay. Thanks, Grandma," she whispered as she bent and placed a kiss against Becky's temple.

She raised her head to see her mother staring at her, and

she quickly averted her eyes when she realized that she had been caught.

"It's time," Kerry announced excitedly, and her father set the time for the countdown.

The voices rose in unison as the excitement crescendoed toward the big finale. "Ten, nine, eight, seven, six, five, four, three, two, one, Happy New Year!"

As the family hugged and cheered, the sound of fireworks erupting in the distance announced the start of yet another journey around the sun.

Cora and her sisters sat on their mother's bed as close as they could get to her and reached over to hug her.

"We love you, Mom. We don't say it enough, but we're happy that we got this time with you, and anything afterward is a blessing that we will cherish," Cora spoke ardently as she pulled away to stare at Becky.

"We're glad you are our mom, and we wouldn't have it any other way," Andrea joined in to say while Jo nodded her agreement.

Becky's light brown eyes glistened with unshed tears as her lips lifted into another smile. "I aaaam h-ha-haappy t-t-to be a-alive t-t-today," tumbled from her mouth.

Jules's heart constricted. It was a sweet and touching moment, but the feeling of melancholy still clung to the air as her family tried to make the most of the situation. Her grandmother was dying— soon.

"We have a surprise for you," Cora said, looking behind her before turning back to her mother with a warm look.

Uncle Luke, who Jules hadn't realized had left, now stood at the door with a large flat object wrapped in brown paper.

Cora rose from the bed as Uncle Luke walked toward her.

"We wanted to give you this for Christmas, but it wasn't ready," Cora explained as she, Andrea, and Jo began removing the paper to reveal a portrait of a younger Becky with her three young daughters surrounding her as they stared adoringly at her.

The room gasped in awe as they stared at the realism of the portrait. Becky was now wearing her oxygen mask, but from the look in her eyes, it was clear that she, too, was in awe.

"Mom, you'll always be in our hearts, and there are so many wonderful memories that we will cherish for the rest of our lives, but Drea, Jo, and I agreed that this portrait captures perfectly one of the happiest moments of our childhood and we want it to remain etched in time to share with our own children and grandchildren." At the mention of grandchildren, Cora's eyes linked with her daughter's. Jules felt soft flutters in her belly, and her hand immediately came up to rest on it as her heart pumped a little faster against her ribcage. Cora averted her eyes to gaze lovingly at her mother once more.

After a few more speeches and hugs, the family filed out of the room to give Becky's nurse the opportunity to check her vitals and get rid of her waste.

Jules found herself back on the cold porch staring up at the red, yellow, and green lights that exploded against the night sky at intervals. They were far less than the explosions from ten minutes ago but beautiful, nonetheless.

Her hands found their way over her stomach as her thoughts went to Noah. She wondered where he was at this specific moment and what time of the day it was there. She wondered if he had gotten the opportunity to celebrate the start of a new year. The soft kick that vibrated against her hand elicited a heavy sigh from her lips.

"I miss your dad so much right now, even though I have no business missing him at all for what he did," she confessed, pain shadowing the slight upturn of her lips. After a few more minutes, she headed inside. Bypassing the living room, where she could still hear her family chatting and laughing away, she headed for her room to try and get some rest.

***

Jules woke with a start after another one of her countless dreams that always ended with Noah's betrayal. She rubbed her tired eyes before allowing her hands to fall by her side as she released a slow breath. Glancing at the digital clock on the night table, her eyes widened in surprise that it was after ten.

The noise from outside her slightly ajar door caught her attention. She tried to remember if she'd closed the door but ended up concluding that Diane, who she was sharing a room with, had probably left it open.

Throwing off the covers, Jules walked over to the door and poked her head outside, watching as members of her family moved back and forth, chattering, some carrying trays of food from the kitchen toward the back door. She pulled her head back inside, closed the door, and headed to the bathroom to prepare for the day.

After her shower, she threw on some leggings and an oversized wool sweater. Uggs on her feet completed her ensemble.

"Good morning, honey. How did you sleep?" Cora greeted her with a bright smile the moment she stepped out onto the porch.

"Good morning. I slept okay," she responded. "What's happening?" she asked, pointing with her chin to the patio where most of the family was talking and laughing, playing games, or stuffing their faces. The smell of charcoal intermingled with the smell of spices and cooked meat filled her nostrils.

"We're having an impromptu family barbecue, themed a winter barbecue. We thought it would be a great way to finish out the first day of the new year," her mother explained.

Jules nodded in understanding as she looked out at the sea of smiling faces. Bright golden rays beamed down on them from a cloudless sky, and she realized that the day seemed warmer despite the few centimeters of ice that still clung to the earth.

Bittersweet Memories

"You can go join them if you want," her mother suggested.

"Yeah," she answered before stepping off. After greeting a few of them, she headed for the table laden with food and drinks. She scooped up some of the tortellini pasta salad onto a plate and added roasted corn. She proceeded to fill a glass with the red punch from the large bowl on the table. She then took a seat in one of the few empty chairs overlooking the water. She rested the plate in her lap and the glass on the smooth surface of a rock sticking out of the snow.

"Hot dog?"

Jules looked past the hand holding the food to see her cousin Kerry grinning down at her. At that exact moment, Jules felt her stomach rumble.

"Thanks," she replied, taking the hot dog from the woman with a grateful smile. She immediately took a bite and moaned in satisfaction.

"Someone's hungry." Kerry chuckled.

"Very," Jules returned. "I guess maybe it's because I'm eating for two now."

Kerry nodded as her eyes skimmed Jules's belly. "How are you holding up?" she asked seriously.

Jules looked away from her and sighed. "Honestly, I'm tired and...scared. Tired and scared."

Kerry lowered herself into the seat next to Jules, and the two stared out at the water. "I know everything might seem like it's out of control and that this isn't what you bargained for, but I want you to know that it'll get better. You know why?"

Jules looked over at her expectantly.

"Because you have the support of your whole family, who would do anything for you. Back when I was pregnant with my first daughter, I was alone and scared, and it made me make some poor choices, choices I regret to this day." Kerry stared out at the water, her face taking on a faraway look.

Jules recalled that she'd ended up giving her baby up for

adoption but by some miracle, she got to reconnect with her daughter.

"How did you do it? How were you able to move on with your life after that?" she asked, anxious for the answer.

Kerry looked over at her, the melancholy in her eyes telling. "It was hard, especially the first couple of months. All I could think about was my baby, wondering if she was okay and if she was being treated well. But, with time, I learned to cope— to continue living life. But I never lost hope."

Kerry released a slow breath that rushed from her lips like smoke before dissipating into the air.

"What I want you to understand is that you're not a failure. Despite what that little voice in your head is telling you, you are strong, and you will get through this. You are also free to make your own choice. That baby growing inside of you is special. Don't let anyone tell you any different."

"Thanks, Kerry. I appreciate the advice," Jules said, and she meant every word.

After Kerry left, Jules dug into the pasta salad, trying to appease the hunger that seemed more evident after she finished the hot dog.

She caught movement from the corner of her eye and turned to see her mother settling into the seat Kerry had vacated. Cora gave her a bright smile as she settled.

"So, have you thought about names for the baby?" she asked after a few minutes of silence.

"No, not yet," she replied.

"I can help you...make a few suggestions that might be helpful."

"Thanks, but no thanks," Jules declined.

Cora's head slowly bobbed in understanding, and she turned to stare out at the water. After a few more minutes of silence, Cora spoke.

"Are you ever going to tell me what happened back in Seoul?"

Jules opened her mouth to say something, but at the last second, she clamped her lips together.

"Jules." Cora sighed tiredly as she stared at her daughter. "How am I supposed to help you if you won't talk to me? You used to tell me everything. Why are you shutting me out? I just want to help," she spoke in earnest.

"That's because I don't want your help," Jules said with steel in her voice.

Jules watched as Cora's eyes widened in surprise. Jules drew in a deep breath and released it as she tried to calm her frayed nerves.

"Mom, I'm not trying to be mean, but I just need some time, please...I need to figure this out on my own." Jules rose to her feet, indicating she was finished with the conversation. After disposing of the paper cup and plate, she headed inside the house, feeling too drained to interact further with anyone of her family members.

As she walked down the hall toward her bedroom, the doorbell rang. Releasing a breath of frustration, she walked into the foyer and pulled the door open to find a young woman with hair as black as midnight and a grin that extended all the way up to her dark green eyes that crinkled at the corner.

"Hello, may I help you?" Jules asked, beaming.

"Hi, I'm Lily, Jamie's daughter," she greeted.

Chapter Six

"This is Erin. You know what to do."

"Erin, this is your mother calling again. Sweetie, I've been trying to get a hold of you for the past four days. Why aren't you responding to my calls or texts? Please call me as soon as you're able to. Love you."

The ragged breath that left Cora's lips deflated her shoulders as the anxiety she'd been feeling about her daughter not returning her calls or messages caused her mind to imagine all sorts of unimaginable things.

Dialing the only other person who could possibly know where Erin was, she brought the phone to her ear as it began ringing.

"Hello?"

"Hi, Brian. It's me, Cora."

"Hi..."

"You can still call me mom, Brian. I still consider you as my bonus son," she encouraged the young man at his hesitation.

"Mom," Brian replied slowly as if testing out the words. "How are you?"

Bittersweet Memories

"I'm fine. Thanks for asking. How are you doing?"

There was a brief pause as the sound of Brian taking in a deep breath and releasing it sounded over the phone. "I've been better, but I can't complain, I guess," he replied.

Cora nodded; her lips pursed as she knew the root of his response. "I know, sweetie. Listen, the reason I called was to ask if you've spoken to Erin in the past couple of days."

"Uh, no, I haven't. I've been trying to get her since New Year's, but her phone goes to voicemail, and she hasn't responded to any of my messages either. Is something wrong?" he asked worriedly.

Cora released a small sigh before replying, "I'm not sure. I haven't heard from her in the same period of time as you, and I have to admit I am a bit worried."

"Yeah. That's not like her," Brian agreed. "If she doesn't respond by later today, I'm gonna head down to Manhattan. She gave me her address."

"Thanks, Brian. I appreciate that." Cora breathed out.

"It's not a problem," the young man assured her.

"I know the breakup hasn't been easy on you, sweetie, but I want you to know that I'm rooting for you, and you'll always be welcome here because I already consider you family."

"Thanks, Mom," Brian said gratefully. "I just wish I knew what changed between us." He sighed. "I thought we were back on track when we left Oak Harbor, and I was working up to the moment to ask her again...we were fine, but then in October, she said it wasn't working out and that we needed to break up. She still hasn't given me a reason, so I don't know what to do to fix it...to fix us." Brian's coarse breath sounded over the receiver.

"Brian," Cora said. "I am truly sorry that this happened to you. I do wish there was something more I could do to help you both," she spoke softly into the receiver. "You guys are going through a rough patch, and it's meant to either break your relationship for good or help you to get onto a brighter, healthier path."

"Thanks, Mom. You don't know how much I needed some reassurance," Brian said with feeling.

Cora's lips turned up in a smile.

"I will always be rooting for you both."

"I know. I'll let you know if I hear from her."

"Thanks, sweetie."

At the end of the call, Cora's mind was far from settled. She dragged the palm of her hands down her face as a worried breath escaped her lips. She pondered booking a flight to New York. She was worried sick.

Erin's life-altering changes had come so suddenly. She'd broken up with Brian and moved out of the apartment they'd shared for two years and quit her job at the advertising agency she'd started her career and was now working as a fashion marketer for one of the biggest fashion companies in the state. It was as if she didn't know her daughter anymore.

"Please let my baby be okay," she whispered prayerfully. Cora made her way to the front door, and after securing her coat and hat, she left the house. As she walked along the snow-covered path, she pondered how her children had ended up in the predicaments they found themselves in and how helpless she felt. Erin had always been the level-headed daughter whose choices always made sense, but now, none of them did, and it seemed she became less predictable with each passing day. While Jules was the opposite of Erin in that she was more impulsive and always spoke her mind, ever since she came back from Seoul, she had been extremely private. Cora sighed, her breath coming out as a puff of smoke. Arriving at the inn, she shook off the snow from her boots and entered the foyer.

"Hi, Cora. I wasn't expecting to see you over here until this afternoon," Marg greeted, walking from behind the reception desk.

"Hi, Marg," she returned. "I thought I'd get a start on the books early and help with whatever needs to be done," she informed her friend and the inn's manager.

"All right. That sounds like something someone bored would say, or someone running away from their problems," Marg surmised, her eyes narrowing on Cora's face. "What's wrong?" she asked.

Cora exhaled, and her shoulders fell, along with her face. "I think I'm a bad mother," she murmured painfully.

"What are you talking about? That's not true," Marg refuted.

Cora looked up at her friend, her eyes sunken with hopelessness.

"Let's talk in the kitchen," Marg advised.

The two women made their way to the small kitchenette and took seats around the table.

"Tell me what happened," Marg urged, placing her hand on top of the one Cora had on the table for support.

"I don't know what's happening in either of my daughters' lives. At least Jules is here, and I can at least keep an eye on her but Erin...she is a different matter. I've been trying to get her since New Year's, but she hasn't been returning my calls."

Marg listened intently, her head moving back and forth in thought.

"I know it's hard, but your daughters are young adults still trying to navigate this world they came to be a part of. They have to take responsibility for their actions and make their own mistakes, and you will have to stand by and let them. Just let them know that you are there for them when they need your help and give them room to choose to come to you for help."

Cora nodded in understanding. "It's just hard not to be needed as much, I guess," she confessed. "I remember when they used to come to me for everything. I suppose I've just been feeling useless as they no longer do."

"They still need you, Cora," Marg encouraged. Cora beamed appreciatively at her friend as she reached over with her free hand to rest atop the one Marg rested on her other hand.

"So, how are things with Ben?" she asked, changing the subject.

Immediately Marg's face brightened with the upturn of her lips. "Things have been going great. Ben's wonderful." She sighed happily.

Cora grinned, satisfied. "I'm happy to hear that." Something flashed through Marg's eyes. It was Cora's turn to ask, "What's wrong?"

"It's nothing, really." Marg waved her off.

Cora gave her friend a pointed look.

Marg looked down at the table, her brows furrowed. "I have been having this feeling that I'd like to have a child of my own," she revealed, staring back at Cora with vulnerability.

"Are you saying you want to have a baby?" Cora carefully asked.

Marg released a heavy breath, covering her forehead as her eyes fluttered shut. "I don't know what I'm saying. It's highly improbable. It was just a thought." She said.

Cora could see the strain behind her eyes. "Marg, if you want to have a child, you shouldn't just cast it aside. This is something very important. Have you talked to Ben about it?"

"No. I haven't," she replied, looking away. "It might just be a passing desire. I'm not definitely sure if that's what I really want. I've just been weighing the odds."

"Okay," Cora responded. "But..."

Marg turned to look at her.

"If this is what you really want, don't push it under the rug. Do what's best for you," she encouraged.

Marg gave her an appreciative smile.

The two women turned toward the sound of the door opening.

"Oh. Good morning. I hope I'm not interrupting."

"No. Not at all, Jennifer," Marg informed the small woman, beckoning with her hand for her to come into the room.

"Good, because I am in need of some coffee." The woman grinned, walking over to the counter to remove a cup, then turned on the percolator.

"Cora, this is Jennifer Kitson, one of our guests that checked in yesterday," Marg introduced. "Jennifer, Cora is one of the owners of the inn along with her two sisters."

"It's a pleasure to meet you, Jennifer," Cora greeted warmly.

"Likewise," the woman replied with a bright, welcoming smile of her own. Her features were elven-like, in Cora's opinion, with high cheekbones, small heart-shaped lips, and slanted eyes set in an oval face. Her brown hair was neatly tucked behind her upturned ears.

"I could have made you a cup if I knew that's what you wanted," Marg spoke up as the woman turned in their direction.

"Nonsense, Marg. I told you I like doing things for myself. I wouldn't have troubled you for something this simple," the woman said.

"I know, and I understand that, but you are a guest, Jennifer."

"At an inn where everything is at my disposal to be able to do for myself."

"I'm gonna head to the office and look over those books," Cora informed Marg, rising to her feet.

"All right, I'll come and find you in a bit," Marg told her.

Cora left the kitchenette and entered the modest office on the opposite side. She sat in the chair behind the small oak desk and opened the ledgers that were already on top of it. After completing the task, she decided to take a stroll back to the main house.

Cora noticed Andrea's parked green Jeep the moment she arrived, and her brows furrowed. She had thought her sister would be out for the whole day as she had left to go to the fire station to assist Donny's squad in using technology in rescue missions. Andrea had mentioned that they would be going on a date after his shift.

She heaved a sigh of relief as she stepped through the front door and placed her jacket in the coat closet. Her heart thumped against her chest, and her anxiety elevated as she made her way down the hall to check on her mother. She paused in the doorway upon hearing her sister's voice.

"I remember I scratched Dad's car because he'd told me more than twice not to drive it. He was so furious, and I was scared he would ground me for life, but then you simply touched his arm and whispered something in his ear, and I don't know, but to me, it was like you had magic because he calmed down almost immediately and apologized for shouting at me. From that day, Mom, you were my hero. I never got to tell you thanks back then, and over the years, I became so angry and bitter that I let go of all the good memories. But I want you to know that I love you, and I have and do appreciate everything you've done for me. You are my hero, Mom."

A tear slipped from Cora's eyes as she watched her sister reach her hand over to rest it on their mother's cheek.

"You are my hero," Andrea repeated as tears flowed down her face, even as she tried to maintain the smile on her lips.

Cora couldn't take it. Clasping her hands over her mouth to prevent the sob threatening to fall from her lips, she quickly pushed away from the door and made her way to her room.

Chapter Seven

Cora wiped the sleep from her eyes as the sound of her vibrating phone pulled her out of her slumber. Rolling over on her side, she reached over and slowly felt along the tabletop, careful not to topple the lamp as she followed the motion of the vibration to her phone. When she found it, she pulled it to her ear.

"Hello," she croaked into the device. Her hand rested on her forehead, and her eyes shuttered.

"Hi, Mom."

Cora's eyes flew open at the sound of her daughter's voice. "Erin?" she asked tentatively.

"Yeah, Mom. It's me. Did I wake you?"

"Um, no, it's fine," Cora brushed off her concern. She sat up in bed before scooting up until her back rested against the headboard. "I've been calling you for more than a week now. Are you okay? Do you need anything? Should I come get you?" She fired question after question at her daughter.

"Mom." There was a short pause before Erin finished, "I'm...fine."

"Are you sure?" Cora asked, unconvinced.

"Yes. I'm sorry I worried you. I just got caught up with work. It's been super busy working on the new campaign. I was actually in Paris for a few days."

"Paris?" Cora's eyes widened in surprise at her daughter's revelation.

"Yeah, I left New York a day before New Year's Eve to get to fashion shows, first in Milan and then Paris. My boss Mark said I needed to be there to draw inspiration from the collections," Erin explained.

"But, Erin, sweetie...why didn't you tell me or someone else that you were leaving the country? I was worried sick that something was wrong, and I didn't know where you were...I called Brian, and he hadn't spoken to you. You can't do that, Erin."

"I know, Mom. I'm sorry." The young woman sighed softly. "Everything happened so fast...I wasn't thinking."

Cora exhaled loudly. "Erin, I know you're an adult, and I respect that you're independent and making your own decisions, but...it worries me that you're becoming so...it feels like you're becoming distant. Are you sure everything's fine?" she pressed, her voice soft and inviting.

There was a short pause and ruffling in the background before Erin spoke. "Everything's fine," she stressed. It sounded as if she was trying to convince herself that it was the truth more than her mother.

Cora's brows positioned downward, and her forehead wrinkled in concern.

"You said you called Brian?" Erin asked, changing the subject.

"Yes. I called him to find out if he'd talked to you, but he said he hadn't."

"Oh," she said simply. "Did he say anything else?" she followed up, her voice bordering on hopefulness.

"He misses you," Cora revealed. "But you already know that."

A heavy breath whooshed through the receiver. "I...I can't think about that right now," came Erin's tense response.

"He loves you," Cora reminded her.

Another sigh left her daughter's lips. "I know," she sadly replied.

"And do you...still love him?" Cora asked. The line grew silent, and she waited patiently for her daughter's response.

"I don't know," came her soft reply nearly a minute after.

Cora's heart squeezed tight at the confusion and fear in her daughter's voice, and at that moment, she wished she was in New York to comfort her and whisper soft words of encouragement that it would all be okay.

"Mom, I have to go. I just called to let you know that I'm fine, but I'm heading out now."

"All right, sweetie," she accepted.

"I'll talk to you later."

"Sure. Erin?"

"Yeah, Mom?"

"I love you..."

"I love you too."

Cora sighed softly as she pulled the phone from her ear. It was clear to her that her daughter was spiraling, and there was nothing she could do to help her...not unless she asked for it. When had the relationship with both her daughter's deteriorated so much? They both needed help, and she wanted to be there for them, but they weren't letting her. She wondered if this was how Becky had felt after she and her sisters left Oak Harbor as young adults all those years ago, cutting off all ties.

She scooted to the edge of the bed and stood. After a long stretch, she made her way to the bathroom to prepare for the new day. Then she threw on some comfy clothes and made her way downstairs and toward the kitchen.

The ringing of the doorbell stopped her, and she turned and walked toward the front door.

"Hey, cuz," Kerry greeted her with a bright smile that caused her brilliant green eyes to shine through like emeralds.

"Hey, yourself," Cora returned. "What're you doing here at five thirty in the morning? Shouldn't you still be in bed getting your beauty rest?" she asked, looking from the imaginary watch on her wrist to her cousin, with a tilt of her head.

Laughter poured from Kerry's lips. "I wish. I'm always up before the crack of dawn. Force of habit, I guess. I also like getting to the bakery early. I do my best thinking there when I'm prepping for the fresh pastries I'll be making," she explained.

"That's a good plan," Cora agreed with a nod.

"I came to drop off some pastries for the eatery. Jo asked me to." Kerry walked over to the low table and lifted the tray she'd rested there. The smell of caramelized brown sugar and sweet cinnamon wafted to Cora's nose. She moved out of the way, allowing Kerry to step into the foyer.

"Jo's still asleep, so you can put them on the island until she comes down," she informed her cousin as they walked into the kitchen.

"Great," Kerry responded, sliding the aluminum tray onto the marble surface of the island. "How's Aunt Becky?" she turned and asked.

Cora's lips sank into a sad smile. "Not much better," she revealed.

Kerry gave her a sympathetic look.

"There's nothing we can do about it, I know, but I just feel...helpless." Cora stared off into the distance, the weight of the words settling like an anvil in her chest.

Kerry walked over to her and placed a comforting hand on her shoulder.

"I try not to think too much about the fact that she doesn't have much time left, but when I'm alone with my thoughts, it's the only thing I can think about along with everything else that's going wrong," she confessed, releasing a defeated breath at the end.

Kerry's hand moved further down until it rested in the middle of her back. She slowly rotated her palm in a soothing motion. After some time, she spoke, "Everyone's been stressed about what's happening to Aunt Becky. I know words aren't enough to express how sad I am that this is happening to you, Drea, and Jo, especially with Uncle Sam gone, but I will always be here for you guys."

Cora turned her head in her cousin's direction and flashed her a grin. Kerry smiled back at her.

"I have an idea. Why don't we have a girls' night out?" she suggested.

Cora's eyes glistened with hesitation, and her lips parted with the intention to decline the offer.

"It'll be fun," Kerry pressed, bumping her shoulder with hers. "Tonight is karaoke night at Sam's Tavern back in Coupeville. I think a little drive out will do us great," she urged.

"Sure," Cora agreed. Maybe a girls' night out would do her well.

Kerry's lips widened in a face-splitting grin.

"What about the others? Do you think they'll be up to it?" Cora asked as she stood by the door with her cousin.

"Leave that part up to me," Kerry advised before turning and making her way down the porch steps and walking down the path to her car.

*　*　*

"Are you sure you don't want to come with, sweetie? It'll be fun."

"I'm sure. I'll be fine. Go have fun."

Cora stood by the living room entrance staring helplessly at the back of her daughter's head as her focus remained on the television.

She had wanted Jules to come on the trip with them and had thought it would have been a good opportunity for them to bond, but Jules wasn't interested, and it left her feeling disappointed. Releasing a soft sigh, she said, "Okay. I'll be back in a few hours. If you need anything at all, call me."

"All right."

"The nurse is with Mom."

Cora watched her daughter for a few more seconds before turning on her heels to join her sisters in the foyer.

"Ready?" Drea asked, looking her over.

Cora plastered a smile on her lips. "Yes. I am."

The trio left the house and piled into Cora's SUV. They would be stopping to pick up Marg before meeting the others in town.

"Hi, girls," Marg welcomed them cheerily as they pulled up.

Cora and the others beamed in greeting as Marg climbed into the car. Soon they were off again.

They met up with Kerry, Tessa, Sharon, and Rhonda and were off again to Sam's Tavern.

The drive to Coupeville wasn't very long, as it took less than half an hour before they pulled into an almost full parking lot of the restaurant and bar.

The first thing Cora noticed the moment they walked into the establishment was how warm it was compared to the chilly winter air from outside. The room was dimly lit by low-hanging rope pendant lamps suspended from the exposed ceiling joists, giving off a diffused orange glow. The bar featured prominently at the far-right corner while the square tables were pushed back against the long black booth chair that took up most of the left wall. Cushioned chairs were situated on empty sides of the table. A number of the tables were already occupied by patrons having their meals and conversing happily.

"Hi, welcome to Sam's Tavern," a perky blond woman greeted them with a bright smile on her lips. "I'm Cindy."

"Hi, Cindy. We'd like a table that can sit our group," Kerry greeted back.

"Sure. Right, this way."

The group followed the woman to two unoccupied tables that stood side by side.

"I'll let you ladies get settled, and someone will come to get your order soon. Also, tonight's our karaoke night. It starts after nine. Feel free to participate and enjoy your time at Sam's Tavern."

"Thank you, Cindy," the woman replied.

The woman left them and made her way toward the bar.

"I don't know about you ladies, but after the week I've had, I think I need a drink," Rhonda gave out, rising from her seat and making her way toward the bar. The group of women exchanged looks of worry as they watched her.

"She's having marital problems but let's not bring it up unless she wants to talk about it," Tessa suggested.

Cora and the others nodded in understanding. She knew the toll marital issues could take on a person. She only hoped it wasn't as serious as what she'd been through and that she and Shawn could work it out. She reached for her menu and perused it.

"Hi, my name is Jason. I'll be your waiter this evening," a young man informed them as he placed glasses of water before them. "Are we ready to order?"

The women spent most of the evening talking about what was happening in their respective lives, some more open than others as they enjoyed their meal.

"Shawn doesn't understand that I need something to do, anything. Natalie and Jordan are gone, and I just feel like I no longer have a purpose. Shawn's been busier than usual, so he doesn't have time for me...I feel like I don't even know him anymore."

Cora's lips turned down into a frown as she listened to her cousin talk about her marriage, which seemed to be falling apart. She wasn't sure she was the right person to give her advice and so she kept her mouth shut, choosing to show her care by just listening to Rhonda vent.

"Have you tried counseling?" Sharon asked. All eyes turned to her, including Rhonda's. "We went through a rough patch in our marriage, but after doing counseling, we've been doing a whole lot better," she explained.

Rhonda looked back at her skeptically. "I don't know..."

"Nothing tried, nothing achieved," Cora found herself butting in to say.

"I'll think about it." The others nodded in encouragement.

Just then, Cora felt a vibration coming from her bag that sat on her lap. Taking out her phone, she realized that it was Jamie calling.

"Excuse me, ladies, I have to take this."

"Don't take too long. Karaoke is about to start," Kerry said, giving her a knowing look.

"Hi," she greeted the moment she stepped out of the building.

"Hi. How's girls' night?" he asked.

"It's going okay," she replied.

"I'm glad. You deserve some time away from the house."

"What do you mean?" she asked, brows drawn together.

There was a short pause before Jamie replied.

"Ever since your mother's gotten worse, you haven't left the house except to go by the inn. I just think a change of setting is a good thing sometimes."

Cora felt her chest tighten as the thought of her mother

lying, unmoving on the bed back home, came rushing into her mind, clouding over the high she'd had not too long ago.

"Yeah, well, when your mother is staring at death's door, it makes it hard to be even remotely happy, especially when you also have to deal with the pain of rejection from your own daughters," she spoke solemnly as a tear slipped down her cheek.

"Shoot, Cora. I'm sorry...I shouldn't have brought it up. I'm just worried about you."

"All right. I gotta go," she spoke softly as hot tears continued to trail down her cold face.

"Cor—"

"The girls are calling me. I'll talk to you later." Cora ended the call, not giving Jamie time to say anything, as she completely broke down in the parking lot. The weight of everything came crashing down on her once more.

Chapter Eight

"So, what we're measuring today is the baby's head, her belly, and her thighs. I also want to check the placenta and the fluid around her to make sure everything is okay so far."

"All right," Jules accepted her doctor's explanation, watching the woman roll the chair she sat on over to her with a tube in her hand. Opening the tube, the woman squirted the content onto Jules's tummy in a circular motion.

Jules shivered the minute the cold gel hit her belly. She would never get used to the feeling, no matter how many times she had to do an ultrasound.

The doctor then switched on the monitor before resting the transducer probe on her stomach, using the flat head to spread the gel.

Jules turned her head to look at the black-and-white image of her baby on the monitor as the pulse-like sound from the monitor filled the room.

"The heartbeat is strong. That's a good sign," the doctor

informed her as she moved the probe around. "That's her head. Can you see her two little eyes?"

"Yes, I do," Jules replied, her lips broadening as she looked at the two black spots that represented the baby's eyes. She marveled at how much more defined her little girl's features were since her last visit, which was just two weeks ago. Every visit, she found herself becoming more attached to her, and it brought another smile to her lips.

She felt a squeeze on her shoulder, and she inclined her head until she met her mother's beaming face.

"Oop, we have a runner," the doctor expressed, pulling Jules from the moment she was sharing with Cora. The two looked at the monitor, and small chuckles left their lips as they watched the baby move around, trying to avoid the probe.

"Look at her little feet...her hands," Cora spoke with awe as she reached over to Jules to point at the monitor. "Oh, she's so adorable. I can't wait to meet her."

This brought another grin to Jules's lips as her chest filled with warmth. She reached up to grasp her mother's hand as they watched the baby move about while the doctor explained what was happening. Cora squeezed her hand encouragingly.

"I'm happy with the progress I'm seeing, but there are some things that I am still concerned about."

Jules's smile dissolved, and her eyes clouded over with fear. She felt her mother give her hand another squeeze as she waited anxiously for the doctor to explain her concerns.

"I see the face you're making, Jules, but I don't want you to be too worried. I promise to do my best to ensure you have a healthy baby," the woman said, smiling in a way that was meant to assuage her fears. It had the opposite effect on Jules, making her more uneasy.

"What is the problem, Doctor Wright?" Cora stepped in to ask.

"There is an abnormal amount of amniotic fluid around

your baby, meaning there's more than what should be there. It might not lead to any major issues, but it can, like preterm labor or an emergency C-section so from now until the baby is due, I'm going to need you to come in once a week."

"Okay," Jules replied timidly.

"Is there anything that she needs to do?" Cora asked, taking charge.

"I just need her to remain stress-free, try to get a lot of rest, and don't try to do any strenuous activities," the woman advised as she wiped the gel from Jules's belly. "Can you do that?" she asked, directing her gaze to Jules.

Jules could only manage a slight nod as her tongue felt heavy and stuck to the roof of her mouth.

"I'm gonna go get the printout of the ultrasound and some paperwork. I'll be right back," the woman explained, rising from her chair and heading for the door.

"How are you feeling?" Cora asked after more than a minute of silence.

"Honestly?" Jules looked back at her mother, tears burning the back of her eyes.

Cora gave her a short nod to continue.

"I'm scared," her voice cracked. Her chest moved up and down rapidly as she tried to regulate the wild beating of her heart.

Cora reached out and placed her palm against her cheek comfortingly. "Everything will be fine," she murmured, trying to set her at ease. Her blue-gray eyes held Jules's lighter blue ones unblinkingly as she willed her to believe it.

Jules's head slowly bobbed back and forth. "Thanks, Mom," she breathed out.

Cora grinned. She took a seat in the chair by the bedside. "You know, when I found out I was pregnant with you, I was so scared."

Jules's eyes snapped to her mother, surprised and questioning. "Why?"

"My pregnancy with Erin had been a roller coaster ride. I was in and out of the hospital. I had morning sickness that lasted up to my third trimester, and to top it off, she was breached. They wanted to do a C-section, but I refused, wanting to birth my baby naturally. It was the worse pain I'd ever felt, and I wanted to crush your father's hand for doing what we had done to me." Cora gave a small chuckle, her head shaking from side to side. "In the end, Erin came, and she was healthy and strong, but it had taken a toll on my body, and I almost died from excessive bleeding."

"Mom," Jules gave out, alarmed.

Cora gave her a reassuring look. "It was a long time ago, sweetie, and I'm fine now."

Jules's face remained pulled tight with concern.

"The doctors wanted me to terminate my pregnancy with you. They said it was risky and that I might not be able to bring you to full term. I thought long and hard about it and decided you were worth the risk."

At her mother's words, a soft upturn of her lips broke out. "How did it turn out?"

A light giggle left Cora's lips. "You're here, aren't you?" she asked, reaching over and sticking a stray strand behind Jules's ear. "I was much sicker with you than I'd been with Erin. They were so convinced that the risk was too great and the possibility of you surviving was slim. I had hope that you would make it out all right, though, because I knew you were a fighter."

Jules's lips quirked up slightly, her eyes filled with wonder as she listened to her mother talk.

"So even though in the end they took you at seven months, I knew you'd make it."

Cora reached over and traced the curve of Jules's cheek to

her chin with her palm. "My miracle baby." She beamed brightly.

Jules reached up to grasp her mother's hand. "Thank you for not giving up hope," she said warmly.

"Always and forever," Cora breathed out, her eyes bright with promise. "You're my baby. I'll never give up on you."

Jules's heart warmed at her mother's endearment. It also put her mind at ease that her baby would be just fine despite the challenges.

"All right, here we go."

The two women looked across the room at the doctor who'd just walked through the door. Jules reached out to take the sonogram from her. Her face relaxed into a grin as she stared at the black-and-white image of her little girl.

"Our next visit will be a week from now, but I want you to call me if you're having any discomfort that feels unnatural, and please, avoid stressful situations," the doctor implored.

"Okay," Jules accepted, her gaze still trained on the sonogram. It was tangible evidence that her baby was fine. She vowed that she would do anything to ensure that it stayed that way.

Cora helped her off the examination table, and the two made their way toward the exit.

"See you in a week," the doctor said, holding the door open for them.

"See you in a week, Doc," Jules returned.

"You hungry?" Cora asked as they made their way through town on their way home.

Jules hadn't thought about the fact that she'd only eaten a muffin and had an iced tea earlier in the day until that moment as her tummy grumbled in response to Cora's question. "I could eat," she said sheepishly.

Cora nodded.

A few minutes later, they were pulling up to the marina.

Bittersweet Memories

Jules took the time to admire the motorboats, the yachts, and other small vessels docked on either side of the boardwalk that jutted out toward the water and along the breakwater walkway. The vessels gently rocked back and forth as the waves undulated beneath their hulls. The bright golden sun rays glinted off their polished surfaces.

A short while later, they took seats outside at The Grand Marlin, a seafood restaurant along the boardwalk that gave them the perfect view of the endless blue-green water and the fleet of unmoving vessels and the people out enjoying a stroll along the boardwalk or getting a bite to eat like them. Although the time was considerably chilly from the cool winter air from inland, Jules was grateful for the covered pergola that protected them from the glare of the sun.

Another ten minutes and their seafood boil had arrived.

"Mhmm, this looks and smells heavenly. I bet it tastes just as great," Cora gave out, and Jules's belly rumbled in agreement, her mouth salivating at the fresh, briny smell of the seafood infused by a buttery scent tickled her nostrils.

Cora reached down to pick up a lobster tail, and Jules followed suit. The tender flesh melted quickly against her tongue.

"You're right. It tastes great," she directed to Cora as she reached for another lobster tail. Just then, she felt a flutter in her belly, and she stopped to rest her hand over the movement as a smile broke out on her lips. Her eyes dove to her hand before she looked up to see Cora staring at her.

"Looks like she likes it too," she explained.

Cora grinned and agreed.

"I was thinking about baby names."

"Okay, what do you have in mind?" Cora asked.

"I like the names Abigail, Emily, and Olivia," she answered.

Cora bobbed her head. "Those are lovely names," she responded, beaming. "Either one or two will be great choices."

Jules nodded her thanks as she delved back into the sumptuous meal before her. An unbidden smirk rolled onto her face as she reflected on how well the day had gone. For the first time since coming to Oak Harbor, it felt as if the relationship was finally mending. She was even considering telling her about Noah and what happened back in Seoul.

At the thought of the man, her mood soured, and the smile slipped from her lips. She thought about how he was missing out on being a father to their little girl. There was already so much he had missed, like the first time she moved, her first response to the food she ate, or when the doctor pointed out that she was a girl. If he hadn't been a lying cheat, maybe he's the one who would have been sitting in the chair opposite hers if he wasn't deployed.

"Are you all right, sweetie?"

She looked up to see her mother staring at her in concern.

"I'm fine," she muttered, not able to muster a smile.

"Are you sure?"

"I'm fine," she repeated with finality.

Cora's eyes widened in surprise before they shuttered.

"I'm ready to go," she said, pushing away from the table and standing.

Wordlessly, Cora stood to her feet and turned in the direction of the parking lot.

The ride home was done in tense silence. Jules felt guilty for the way she'd snapped at her but couldn't bring herself to apologize as Noah remained predominantly on her mind.

Chapter Nine

"Hi, can I come in?" Jules asked as she pushed open her grandmother's door to look in.

"Yes, of course," the nurse who stood by Becky's bedside, facing her direction, responded. Small lines crinkled at the corners of her mouth and the sides of her eyes. "I just finished cleaning her feeding tube." She held up a surgical tray with gauze and small medical tools and a small pail in Jules's line of vision as she said this.

"Okay," Jules replied. She moved further into the room as the small but wiry woman rounded the bed and moved toward the door. Jules moved away, giving her the space to exit.

"It's really nice that you try to spend time with your grandmother. She needs it... especially now," the nurse said as she looked over her shoulder at Becky before turning to give Jules a kind smile. Jules returned it before watching her leave.

"Hi, Grandma," she spoke softly as she came to a stop by the bed. Becky's eyes slowly opened and shifted in her direction.

"I brought that book I promised I'd get for you," Jules said, holding up the book for the woman to see. "The Memoirs of an Appreciative Life." She brought the book down to read the title before training her eyes on her grandmother once more.

After taking a seat by the bed, she opened the book and began to read. "What does it truly mean to live? Is it looking back at the end with a smile on your face and the confidence that there are no regrets? Is it knowing that you have made an impact on the lives of those whom you hold dearly, knowing that you have left them with the best tools to continue traversing this path of becoming more than just another human being taking up space on earth?"

As she continued to read the book inspired by a true story, she occasionally glanced up to see her grandmother's eyes focused on her. Jules's lips turned up in an endearing grin each time, but her heart remained heavy with unbridled sadness. The woman who had appeared so strong and in control just over a year ago now required someone to move her from one spot on her bed to the next. She had a feeding tube running from her side, and an oxygen mask lay atop her chest. A soft pillow propped up her legs and was being used to prevent the heels of her feet from bruising. Becky had lost a significant amount of weight. She was next to skin and bones. There was nothing she nor the rest of the family could do as they watched the woman wither away before their very eyes. The doctor had warned them of what to expect now that she was transitioning to the final stage of her ALS, but it was still hard to watch. She didn't think any forewarning could have prepared them to see this.

Her mother and aunts put on brave faces, but she could see it in the furtive glances, the slipped smiles when they thought no one was looking, the stiffness in their shoulders, and the whispered conversations. They were suffering, and so was the rest of the family.

"Life is a gamble. Some win and some d..." Jules inhaled

deeply through her nostrils and slowly released it through her lips. She snapped the book shut and looked up at her grandmother, whose eyes were already on her. Even though Becky was unable to string a sentence together, her eyes bore into Jules, examining her. She could sense the question her grandmother wanted to ask her.

"I wish we could go back to a time when everything was simple." She sighed. Jules sat unmoving for more than five minutes, the only sound in the room coming from the beeping monitor. "I never got to tell you about the baby's father, did I?" she broke the silence. "His name is Noah, and we met one day while I was in Seoul with my friends. I ran into him, literally, and went flying, but he caught me before I could fall flat on my bum. I guess you can say the rest was history after that." Her lips turned up in a grin as she went back to that moment. Those first few months had been the lightest she'd felt in a long time. "We were inseparable, but then he was deployed, and I found out I was pregnant." Her lips turned into a frown as she continued. "I called his parents, but a woman answered, claiming to be his fiancée. I was...heartbroken...confused..." Her brows fought to meet as her forehead tightened.

Jules released her lower lip from between her teeth as a soft wind rushed through. Her shoulders deflated. The pain gripped her, shredding her heart as she relived the moment as if it had just happened. She brought her hand up to swipe the moisture she felt at the corner of her eye.

"I had this idea in my head that when he came back to Seoul, we would have picked up where we left off because it already felt like we'd known each other for years. I had a strong connection with him..." she trailed off, staring blankly at the wall across from her grandmother's bed. "I thought he felt it too." She sighed dejectedly. "I was such a fool." She whispered the last part, staring at her hands now clasped in her lap.

"I'm sorry, Grandma. I came in here to keep you company

and maybe bring some joy to you, but instead, I came and offloaded my burden on you." She looked up at her grandmother, her blue eyes apologetic. Becky's light brown ones registered understanding before they fluttered shut.

Jules felt really bad for taking the time to focus on herself and her problems instead of Becky.

Slowly, she rose from her chair, careful not to disturb her, and made her way toward the door. She made a beeline for the kitchen. When she was close enough, she could smell the rich aroma of coffee diffusing into the atmosphere, and when she finally stepped into the room, her eyes engaged with her mother's.

"Hi, sweetheart," Cora beamed.

"Hi," Jules responded with a sheepish look as she walked further into the kitchen and took a seat around the kitchen island.

"Would you like some peppermint tea?" Cora offered.

"Sure. Yes, thanks," she accepted.

Cora nodded before turning to the kettle to prepare her beverage. "I didn't offer you coffee because too much caffeine isn't good for the baby," Cora explained, looking over her shoulder at her daughter.

Jules nodded in understanding but replied, "The doctor says I can have a cup a day."

Cora turned and placed the steaming cup before her. "I know what the doctor said, but sometimes it's better not to chance it." She pulled out one of the high stools opposite Jules and sat with a mug of the caffeinated beverage.

Jules opened her mouth to counter her mother's words but quickly snapped it shut, remembering that she hadn't been particularly pleasant to her the other day, snapping at her when she'd asked her if she was okay.

"Nurse Willis said you were sitting with Mom. How was it?" Cora raised the cup to her lips, the steam from the mug rising and swirling around her face as she sipped lightly while watching her daughter.

"It was..." Jules paused, trying to find the right words to say. "I'm happy that we still have time to spend with her, but I'm sad that she is the way she is now and that the time left is pretty short." She sighed, staring at the brown liquid in her cup. She looked up to see a sad, knowing look on her mother's face.

"I know it's hard, but what matters now is making as many memories as possible we can with her," Cora spoke before pursing her lips thoughtfully.

Jules gestured her understanding.

The two sat for a while, lost in their own thoughts as they continued to drink their hot beverages.

"Mom," Jules started hesitantly.

Cora looked back at her expectantly.

"About yesterday at the restaurant...I'm sorry I snapped at you. I was upset about something, and I took it out on you. You didn't deserve that because you were very helpful and there when I needed you," Jules apologized.

Cora's lips lifted in acceptance. "Thank you for that. I appreciate it. I want you to know that I'm here for you whenever you want to talk."

Jules gave her a look of acknowledgment.

The two sat in comfortable silence, finishing their beverages.

"I'm gonna go check on Mom and then head into town to get some things. Wanna tag along?"

Jules shook her head. "I'm not feeling particularly up for a town visit," she answered. Cora nodded in understanding.

After the two finished, Cora cleared their cups, and Jules made her way to her room. As she stared at her reflection in the mirror, her hands came up to rest against her belly in a loving and protective gesture.

"You are the most precious gift," she whispered lovingly as

she gently rubbed her bulge. The baby reacted almost instantly, kicking against her palm.

"I just wish your dad wasn't such a jerk," she spoke regrettably. Sighing, she turned and made her way to her bed to take a short nap. Her phone pinged, and she picked it up from the table and swiped it open. It was a message from her friend back in Seoul. Her heart skipped a beat as she nervously clicked it open.

"*Hi, Jules. How are you? I know we haven't spoken in a while, and it's pretty late, but Happy New Year. Better late than never, right? School's been great so far. We all miss you and wish you were here with us...Hopefully, when I'm finished over here, I could visit...*"

A smile graced Jules's lips as she read her friend's message. It warmed her that her friends missed her, and although she knew that there was at least one person who wasn't too cut up over her no longer being there, she felt good that Katie made contact.

Noticing another text from her friend, she scrolled and clicked on it to read it.

"*I did something crazy. I really hope you won't be upset with me and that after you find out what it is that I can still visit you. PS I love you, Jules. You'll always be my bonus sister.*"

Jules's brows scrunched up in confusion, not knowing what Katie could have possibly done that would make her mad at her. Her mind went in every direction, and her heart slammed against her chest. There was no way her friend would betray her trust like that. Even though they hadn't spoken in a while and she had, in fact, been distancing herself from everything that reminded her of her broken dreams and aspirations, there was no way Katie could have done that to her.

She hoped.

Chapter Ten

Cora's muscles screamed out as she worked hard to keep her form and control. As her legs widened and her feet hit the tarmac, she pumped her arms back and forth, the force helping to propel her forward. The air squeezed out of her lungs and whooshed through her lips like puffs of smoke.

Although it was relatively very early, quite a number of cars passed her to and fro, a few honking their horns in recognition. On SE Pioneer Way, she followed the long pavement with walkways that led to businesses that were still shuttered, but quite a number of people were still out and about. She passed parents with their children making their way to the elementary school a few meters away. She passed a few men in suits, briefcases in their hands, and a cell at their ear as they walked briskly along the path. She was already a good distance from the house but decided to turn onto SE City Beach St. and headed for Windjammer Park as the adrenaline pumped in her veins.

Cora ran along the shoreline, avoiding the countless pieces of driftwood that littered the beach.

After another ten minutes of running, she slowed her pace until she came to a full stop. Her chest moved up and down in rapid succession as she drew air in and out of her nose. Her breathing settled into a steady rhythm and her lungs no longer felt as if they were catching on fire.

She hadn't noticed how cold it was while running, but now that she had de-escalated, she was hyperaware of just how cold it was. The snow had long since melted, but that didn't stop the biting wind that scraped against her skin, causing the tiny hairs at her nape and along her arms to rise along with goose pimples along the ridges of her skin.

She ran her palms up and down her arms, allowing the friction from her movements to generate enough heat to warm her skin. She turned to face the ocean watching as the waves crashed against each other as they raced to the shore and fizzled out as white foams before receding. She stood there by the shore for a while, taking in the ebb and flow of the water's current and watching the sun gradually rise into the sky, its golden rays creating a dazzling reflection on the surface of the water.

Slowly, her thoughts shifted from admiring the beauty of nature before her to the problems that had pushed her to leave the house for a run. Becky was knocking on death's door, and there was nothing that she or anyone could do about it. She didn't think she would ever be able to accept that, even when the day finally came. She was unsure of what Jules's plans were for her future as she didn't tell her much. She had been afraid to broach the subject as she had realized from early on that those kinds of questions always put her daughter on the defensive. She didn't even know if the father of the baby was aware of the fact that Jules was pregnant. She was also scared of the fact that she was about to become a grandmother. Then there was Erin. Their last conversation had left Cora more worried than she had been those couple of days she hadn't been able to get in touch with her. Her daughter, who'd always been the practical one with a set plan of how she wanted her life to turn out, seemed to have abandoned it all and had no idea what she wanted anymore. It was as if she was making up the script as she went along.

Cora shivered, not because of the cold but because she was scared— scared of the inevitable, scared of the unknown.

Cora closed her eyes and crossed her hands over her chest as she recited the words she'd learned from her mother when she was a child, "Grant me the serenity to accept the things I cannot change, courage to change the things I can and wisdom to know the difference." She reverently repeated the words again. "Grant me the serenity to accept the things I cannot change, courage to change the things I can, and wisdom to know the difference," and another time.

Cora slowly opened her eyes and released a heavy breath as her shoulders sagged in disappointment. She didn't feel any closer to accepting what was happening in her family than she had a few minutes ago, and she definitely didn't know what it was that she needed to do to fix any of it.

Cora turned and made her way unhurriedly up the shore before taking off in a sprint. It didn't take long for her body to adjust to her rhythm from earlier as she retraced her steps on her trek home.

The sound of a horn honking caused Cora's steps to falter. The sound was coming from right behind her and was enough for her to realize someone was trying to get her attention. A blue Tacoma came to a stop along the side of the road before her. She instantly recognized who it was. Her heart thumped wildly. It slammed more forcefully against her ribcage as she watched the tall, muscular man step out of his truck in a pair of blue jeans and a denim jacket covering his broad shoulders.

Her breath caught in her throat when he turned to face her. His eyes trapped her in their onyx depths, and a grin played at the corners of his mouth. She remained transfixed as she watched him shut the van door and walk toward her. The wind tousled his slicked-back raven hair, and a few strands brushed against his left brow.

"Hi," Jamie greeted affectionately when he was finally standing before her.

"Hi," Cora responded, her voice coming out in a breathy whisper.

"If I knew you were running today, I would have joined you," he said, taking in her outfit.

Cora beamed sheepishly. "I just needed some time to clear my head," she informed him.

Jamie nodded in understanding. "Is everything okay?" he asked. His eyes bore into her, searching.

"I'm...better," she replied.

Jamie opened his mouth as if to say something but slowly closed it as he continued to stare at her.

Cora averted her eyes, feeling open before his perceptive gaze.

"Where are you headed?" she asked in an attempt to change the subject. She looked over at the truck before setting her questioning gaze on him.

Jamie looked back at his vehicle before looking at her. "I'm headed over to the inn. I'm working on completing the new gazebo," he explained.

"Oh, that's great," Cora expressed.

"Yeah," Jamie replied, his gaze still fixed on her face. "Are we still on for our date this weekend?"

Her eyes widened in surprise. It had completely slipped her mind. She didn't think now was a good time for that, especially with everything going on. "Jamie," she started, preparing to let him know her thoughts. However, her lips clamped shut at his look of apprehension.

"Yes, I remember our date. I can't wait," she assured him, plastering a grin on her lips.

Jamie didn't respond, but he continued to stare at her, his brows furrowed in concentration. Cora squirmed under the scrutiny. Finally, his gaze dropped as he released a heavy breath, his broad shoulders deflated.

"Cor...what's wrong?" he asked softly, his voice coaxing her.

"What do you mean?" she asked, taking a step back in retreat.

Jamie's gaze went to her feet before looking back at her face. Cora hugged her chest, and she stared nervously back at him.

"You're distancing yourself...from me," he concluded with a slight shake of his head.

A gasp escaped her lips as she widened. "That's not...I'm not," she replied barely above a whisper. Her gaze darted away from his perceptive eyes as she knew they both knew the truth despite her protest.

Jamie released another sigh. "I know you feel that you have to be strong for everybody, and I admire that about you, Cor... but I also want you to know that you can show your weakness to me because I want to be strong for you. I want to be your protector...the one you trust enough to let see your true emotions."

She felt the warmth of his large hand against her cheek, and her eyes turned to his face. Jamie looked back at her with a mixture of love and concern.

"I need you to trust me that I will protect you no matter what," he implored.

Her heart constricted with guilt. "I'm trying," she responded with an apologetic sigh.

Jamie didn't respond. Unexpectedly, his hand fell from her face, and she instantly missed the warmth from having it there, but just as quickly, Jamie pulled her into his arms and hugged her against his chest.

"I love you," he breathed against her hair.

Cora smiled sadly. "I love you too."

"I'm ready to face everything with you," he reiterated. "You only have to let me in."

They stood along the side of the road wrapped in each other's arms for another minute, the only sound between them, the breath escaping their lungs and the steady rhythm of his heart that she could hear because her ear was pressed against his chest. She felt safe in his embrace like this. The noise in her head lessened until it was just dull drumming. She welcomed the reprieve he offered, but she also knew it wouldn't last because the minute she raised her head off his chest and stepped back, the noise would return.

"Ready to go?" he asked after they separated.

"No. You go ahead. I need to finish my run," she informed him. Noting his hesitation, she gave him a reassuring look. "I need to do this."

"Okay," he said softly, his lips pursed in reluctance. He bent his head and placed a kiss on her forehead before looking back into her eyes. "I'll see you later."

Cora nodded. She looked up at him as he stepped away from her before turning and heading for his truck. As soon as the vehicle drove off, her smile slipped, and she heaved a heavy sigh.

She started her run once more, but her mind was now bombarded by all that Jamie had said to her. She loved him very much, that much she was sure of, but she wasn't sure she was ready to bombard him with all of her problems.

He had proven continually that he was in this for the long haul, and she'd thought she was right there with him. But with each passing day and with the addition of new complications in her life, she didn't think it was fair to chuck all of her problems and insecurities on him. He hadn't given her any reason to believe he wasn't able to manage the heavy stuff in their relationship. It just felt as if it was too soon. She remembered how she'd relied heavily on Joel for emotional support and how after a time, it had seemed as if it had become a burden for him to sit and listen to her fears and concerns. Over time she'd bottled her feelings. The ones she wasn't able to manage on her own, she'd compartmentalized. That's how their marriage had worked for a long time.

At that moment, the realization hit her like a bucket of ice water— she was afraid that her burdens would become a nuisance to Jamie as they'd become to Joel, and she was afraid of having another relationship like the one she had before.

By the time she'd made it back to the house, she was contemplating calling a time-out in their relationship, at least until she could get some things under control.

Chapter Eleven

"What about this one? I think it would look nice on you. You should try it."

Jules's brows furrowed as she stared at the tent dress her cousin held out to her. She liked the daffodil floral prints running all over the dress, but she wasn't sure about the cut of the dress.

"As cute as...that looks, I'm not sure it will look flattering on me, especially in my current state," she replied, pointing to her protruding stomach.

Diane looked from the dress she held up to Jules's belly and then back to the dress, her hazel eyes contemplative. After a few more seconds of scrutiny, she agreed, "You're right. I don't know what I was thinking," she replied, putting the dress away.

"You'd look way better in this one." Jules looked across to where her other cousin, Nikki, stood, holding up a royal blue maxi dress.

This dress Jules could definitely rock. "I like it," she said, taking it from her cousin.

"Good. You can go try it on, and Diane and I will be the judge of how it fits," Nikki suggested.

Jules's eyes filled with apprehension. "I don't think that's necessary," she spoke hesitantly. While she'd agreed to go shopping with the women to get to know them better and bond, she hadn't anticipated that they would be dress shopping, especially not for her. She knew she needed a few items because most of her clothes were either too tight or couldn't fit her at all. She'd noticed that it wasn't just her tummy that had gained weight, but her hips had become much wider, and her arms and legs felt and looked meatier. The pregnancy weight was making her self-conscious, and the thought of people scrutinizing her didn't sit well with her.

"Oh, come on, Jules, it's not like we're going to poke fun at you for the baby weight. We just want to see how well it fits. That way, we can avoid making a trip back to the store if it doesn't fit. Right, Dee?" Nikki turned to Diane for confirmation.

"Um, I think it will look great on you whether you choose to try it on now or later," Diane deflected, giving Jules an encouraging smile.

Jules gave her cousin an appreciative grin of understanding. "I'm not gonna try it then. I'm sure it'll fit," she said, looking directly at Nikki.

Nikki made a face and began to walk off. "You guys are no fun. I'm going to go look in the size zero section for something that'll look great on me. Who am I kidding? Anything I pick out will be great."

Jules and Diane watched their cousin march in the direction of the line of clothes for size zeros.

"I'm sorry about her," Diane turned to Jules and apologized. "She can be a little..."

"Conceited? Catty?" Jules quipped.

Diane chuckled. "Yeah, those are the words I was looking

for," she added. "I didn't think it through when I chose to invite her, but everyone else was busy, and I really wanted you to have a girls' day out. You've been cooped up in the house for too long. You need fresh air and some company around your age," she expressed.

"You're so nice," Jules marveled.

Diane gave her a weird look.

Jules rushed to explain. "What I mean is you didn't have to choose to try and cheer me up, but I am grateful." Jules's lips lifted at the corners.

Diane looked at her seriously. "We're family, Jules. Family should stick together no matter what." At her latter statement, her gaze darted in the direction of their cousin Nikki before turning to settle on her.

"You're right," she agreed with a grin that dimmed after a few seconds as her thoughts went to her sister.

"Come on. Let's go to another store where they have more comfortable-looking clothes," Diane suggested.

Jules nodded in agreement as she switched her thoughts back to the present. The two women walked out of the store with a sullen-looking Nikki lagging behind them. The next store they entered was a sports and casual clothing store. Jules was grateful when she realized that most of what they sold could be classified as baggy and would fit so as not to bring too much attention to her protruding belly.

"So, you're getting married?" Jules asked Diane, looking down at the glittering diamond on her ring finger.

Diane's gaze dropped to the jewelry on her finger before she looked up at Jules. Her gaze had softened, and her lips turned up in a happy smile. "Yeah," she answered. She brought her hands up to her chest, and her index and thumb played with the ring on her finger. "It's not for another six months, but I can't wait." Her smile broadened.

Jules beamed. "I'm happy for you."

"Let's hope Derek can remember the date for his wedding and won't leave you jilted at the altar," Nikki chimed in. "We all know how busy he is, and he can be a bit forgetful at times," she continued with a smug slide of her mouth.

The smile on Diane's face slipped, and the brightness in her eyes waned. "I have faith in Derek, Nikki. He is, after all, my fiancé," she returned with a strained look. Nikki's eyebrow rose in a slow arch, and her lips turned up challengingly.

Diane averted her gaze, and Nikki smirked triumphantly.

The air was thick with tension. Jules looked between Nikki and Diane. She felt uncomfortable with the direction of the conversation, and it was evident that Nikki's words had affected Diane a lot. She wasn't sure what was Nikki's problem, but if she had to guess, it was evident that Nikki was jealous of Diane. Either that, or she was just downright a hurtful person.

"I'll be in the sea of guests cheering you guys on," Jules said, breaking the silence, then touching Diane's upper arm encouragingly. "That's if I get an invite."

"Of course, you get an invite," Diane responded. A look of appreciation crept onto her face, and Jules beamed back.

Jules ended up buying a few sweats and some baggy shirts before they left the store. Nikki whined about how bored she was with not finding the perfect outfit for her upcoming audition for a part in an advertisement.

Diane and Jules exchanged knowing looks before simultaneously mouthing the word "diva." They burst out in laughter. Nikki turned and stared at them suspiciously. They gave her tight-lipped grins before continuing down the corridor of the mall.

The smell of food infiltrated Jules's nostrils, causing her belly to grumble. She'd only eaten some oatmeal and an apple earlier in the day, so it was definitely time to get something to satiate her hunger.

"Can we stop and get something to eat?" she asked as soon as the food court came into sight.

"Now?" Nikki asked, narrowing her eyes.

Movement in her periphery halted her response, and her head moved up to notice a pregnant woman waving in their direction. Jules squinted her eyes, trying to determine if it was actually their attention she was trying to get. Her eyes widened with surprise when she realized who it was.

"I know that woman," she expressed. Her cousins turned, following her line of view. "That's Janice, Donny Hasgrove's daughter-in-law," she explained.

"Donny, as in the man our aunt is dating?" Nikki asked.

"Yeah," Jules confirmed. "I think she's waving us over."

"Let's go say hi then," Diane proposed.

The three women made their way over to her.

"Hi, Janice," Jules greeted when they were directly in front of her.

"Hi, Jules," she returned, beaming before turning her eyes to the other two, "And Diane, if I remember correctly."

"That's right," Diane confirmed.

Janice beamed, pleased. "I'm sorry, I don't remember yours. Names can be a bit tricky for me," she explained, giving Nikki an apologetic look.

"That's fine. I'm Nikki," she replied with a tight-lipped smirk.

"So, I notice we're twinning at this stage," Janice said, looking from her rounded belly to Jules's. "How far along are you?"

"I'm just about seven months," Jules answered.

"Same," Janice replied with a broad grin. "You guys want to join me for lunch?" she asked, throwing the question out to the others.

"No thanks," Nikki answered immediately.

"Um, what she meant is we won't be eating until after

we've finished shopping," Diane jumped in, giving the woman a sheepish look. "Jules can stay with you, though. I know she's tired and would love to get something to eat," she added.

Jules turned to look at her cousin, who smiled back at her encouragingly. "We'll catch up with you a little later," Diane assured her.

"Uh, okay," she agreed hesitantly.

Diane and Nikki wheeled out of the food court and continued down the corridor before disappearing into a shoe store.

"So, what would you like? My treat."

Jules turned to see Janice staring expectantly back at her. She opened her mouth to decline the offer, but Janice jumped in to say, "Next time we meet, you can pay for both our meals."

After another second of hesitation, she acquiesced. "All right. You choose. I'm not fussy."

Janice ordered them two chicken club sandwiches with a side order of potato wedges, an iced tea for herself, and a strawberry milkshake for Jules. They went and took their seat while they waited for a server to bring their order.

"So, do you know the sex of your baby, or is it a surprise?" Janice asked Jules.

"It's a girl," Jules replied, beaming.

"I don't know if it's coincidence or fate, but I'm having a girl too," Janice said with a grin.

"That's wonderful," Jules expressed.

"Yeah. Maybe when they're old enough, we can schedule play dates, and who knows, maybe they'll become best friends," Janice spoke, her tone hopeful.

"That would be nice," Jules agreed.

Just then, their food arrived. Jules readily took a bite of her sandwich, humming in satisfaction as her tongue rolled over the smoky flavored meat, the melted cheese, and seasoning along with the garlic bread as the flavors and textures mixed. "This is really good," she mused.

"I know. It's one of my guilty pleasures," Janice explained.

The two women continued to enjoy their meal while maintaining small talk. This was nice, Jules thought. Even though it was the first pregnancy for the both of them, Janice had been giving her a lot of tips on coping, and she was grateful for it.

"So, have you started birthing classes as of yet?"

"Uh, no. Is it mandatory?" Jules asked.

"No, it isn't mandatory, but it is beneficial," Janice explained. "I started last month, and I've learned a lot so far, such as the early signs that my body is preparing for labor. I'm learning breathing techniques to help me relax. I've used that a bit because I've been having minor Braxton-Hicks contractions, nothing too serious, but the exercises helped."

Jules nodded with interest as she concentrated on the woman's words.

"These classes also help you to determine the best labor position to help the baby line up with your pelvis and when to request pain medication."

"That's a lot to take in," Jules marveled.

Janice nodded in agreement. "It helps to have your partner there with you, so if you forget anything, he's able to remind you. Plus, it's nice to get a free tummy rub now and again." She said.

Jules averted her gaze. "Um, the father isn't in our lives at this time," she breathed out.

"That's fine. You can take someone else. Anybody you choose," Janice assured her.

Jules lifted her head to see the woman's blue eyes shining with compassion.

"So, have you started shopping for baby clothes?" the woman asked, changing the subject.

"No, not yet."

Jules remained in the food court with Janice for over an hour, talking until her cousins showed up.

"Ready to go?" Diane asked.

"Yes," Jules replied, rising to her feet. "Janice, I'm really glad I ran into you. This was a great and informative lunch date." She smiled down at the woman.

"I enjoyed your company too," Janice replied.

The women left the food court and made their way toward the escalator. Just as she was about to step onto the descending steps, she caught the side profile of a man entering a sports store. Her heart slammed against her chest as a wave of familiarity washed over her. *It couldn't be.* She shook her head to clear the fog from her brain and looked back up, but the man had already entered the store. She turned and took a step in the same direction.

"Jules, what are you doing?" Diane called out to her, breaking her focus.

She looked at the store before looking back at her cousins, staring expectantly back at her. "Nothing," she replied with a small grin and walked back to the steps. The three women stepped onto the escalator and allowed it to transport them to the downstairs lobby.

As she sat in the back of Diane's car, she looked back at the mall, her mind running with thoughts of the man she'd seen.

"It can't be him," she whispered desperately.

Chapter Twelve

"How was your time at the mall?" Cora greeted Jules with an expectant smile the minute she stepped through the door.

"It was okay," Jules replied, eyeing her mother warily. "Were you seriously waiting to ask me about how my day went?"

The answer was written in her eyes. "I wasn't just standing here for hours waiting to ask you that question, no. But I was looking out for your cousin's car so that I could ask you, yes."

Jules sighed exaggeratedly. "Mom, you're acting like I'm a kid, and this was my first day at elementary school. It's not," she chided. "We just went to the mall, got some stuff, and talked a bit. That's it."

"I know you might not see it as a big deal, but for me, it is. My cousins and I were very close when we were younger, but life happened, and we drifted apart. I just thought it would be great if you could bond with their children, build a relationship like what your aunts and I are doing," Cora spoke seriously. Her eyes begged Jules to understand.

Bittersweet Memories

"I like Diane. She's very nice," Jules replied conciliatorily.

Cora's lips crawled up into a grin, her eyes shining with satisfaction. "What about Nikki?" she pressed.

Jules thought a little about her answer before responding, "She is...interesting."

Cora's blue-gray eyes stared questioningly at her daughter as her head angled to the side.

"I'm gonna go take a five. I'm beat," she said, cutting the conversation short.

"Okay, sweetie. I'm gonna check in on Mom and head by the inn for a bit," Cora replied.

Jules nodded before heading for her room. After placing the two shopping bags by the door of her closet, she turned and flopped onto the bed. Her body bounced a few centimeters off the bed before settling against the firm mattress. "I'm so sorry for being so rough, my angel," she spoke in a hushed tone as she ran her hand soothingly over her raised tummy. "Mommy doesn't think sometimes." The exhaustion of the day caught up with her shortly, and she dozed off.

When she got up, she went to the bathroom to wash the sleep from her eyes and made her way to the kitchen to find something to eat. She found her mother in the kitchen cooking. The smell from the pot caused her to salivate.

"Hey. Are you hungry, honey?" Cora asked.

Jules gestured yes.

"Good, I'll be finished in about five minutes." She turned back to the stove and lifted the cover off the pot before using the wooden spook in her hand to stir the content.

"It smells great," Jules complimented, taking a seat around the island.

"It's shrimp scampi pasta," Cora called over her shoulder.

"Where's everyone?" she asked after a few seconds of watching her mother work.

"Drea is by the fire station, and Jo is still working at the restaurant," Cora replied. She reached up and removed two dishes from the cupboard and plated the food.

"Can I take this with me to the living room? I wanted to catch up on my favorite TV show." Jules looked expectantly at her mother, who'd just slid the steaming plate before her.

"Uh, sure," Cora agreed.

"Thanks, Mom." Swiping the plate, she made her way to the living room.

"I'll bring in a glass of juice shortly," Cora called after her.

Jules settled on the couch and released a sigh of contentment. After turning the TV to her program, she speared a few strands of the pasta and twined it around to take up a reasonable portion, and brought it to her lips.

Her head spun in the direction of the ringing doorbell.

"I'll get it!" Cora said.

Jules turned her attention back to the television.

"Jules, there's a young man at the door looking for you," Cora told her.

Jules's head snapped up, and her heart skipped a beat. Slowly, she rose to her feet.

"It can't be him...it can't be him," echoed in her head as her feet, now feeling as if they had been cast in cement, moved heavily against the floor, bringing her toward the front door.

Cora was blocking the person, so Jules couldn't make out who it was, but at the sound of her approach, her mother turned in her direction and, at the same time, shifted away from the person.

Her heart tried to claw its way out of her chest, and it felt like a ball of wool had been lodged in her throat.

Noah stood at the door with an unreadable expression before his gaze traveled lower and settled on the bulge made even more prominent by the small blouse barely keeping it contained. His eyes finally dragged back up to her face, and she could see in his eyes a mixture of surprise and questions as they bore through her.

Instinctively, she felt the need to raise her hands to cover her belly protectively, but her hands remained stiff by her sides.

"Why don't you come inside so that the two of you can talk?" Cora invited, breaking the awkward silence that had ensued. "Jules, why don't you take your guest to the living room to talk privately?" Jules was grateful for the reprieve and quickly averted her gaze.

"Okay," she managed to slip through her lips.

"Thank you, Miss..."

"I'm Cora, Jules's mother," Cora informed the young man with a smile of reassurance. "Just call me Cora," she repeated in its not-up-for-discussion tone.

"Thanks, Cora. I'm Noah McKinley," he introduced himself, holding out his hand to Cora.

"Nice to meet you, Noah," Cora greeted back, shaking the hand he offered. "I'll let you two get to it," she said after releasing his hand.

Jules turned wordlessly toward the living room, and Noah followed. Cora stared at the retreating backs of the two young people with knowing eyes.

As soon as they entered the living room, Jules picked up the remote and paused the TV. She stared at the unmoving characters for some time as she tried to collect her thoughts and get her erratic heart under control. Slowly, she turned to face Noah to see him already glaring back at her. His gaze lowered to her belly once more before coming back to her face, his own face taut with determination.

"Is it mine?"

"What are you doing here?" Jules deflected. "How did you even know where to find me?" Her eyes narrowed in anger.

"Your friend Katie back in Seoul gave me your address after

I came looking for you and realized you had disappeared without a trace," he answered.

"It couldn't have been without a trace if you were able to track me down," Jules replied, her voice dripping with sarcasm.

Noah ignored her comment. "It took me a week to wrestle the information out of her."

"I suppose I should applaud her for lasting so long against someone like you," she quipped.

Noah's eyes squinted together. "What's that supposed to mean?"

Jules deflected again. "Why are you here, Noah?"

Noah stared at her for a long time, searching. Jules pulled her cardigan closed over her belly, trying to prevent herself from squirming under his scrutiny.

"Why didn't you call my parents as I told you to?"

"I didn't know I was obligated to," she retorted.

Noah released a tired sigh and raked his hand over his buzz cut. She should have known it was him at the mall. There was no way that it could have been anyone else. Even with his usual brown curls, he still looked like the same Noah from back in Seoul— her Noah. She shook her head to rid herself of those dangerous thoughts.

"I thought we had something special between us," he spoke in earnest.

Jules stared at him in incredulity before laughter burst from her lips. "Is that what you're calling what we had? You're even more delusional than I ever thought possible." She shook her head in disbelief.

Noah's eyes widened in surprise before he stared at her as if he didn't know her.

"I don't know what happened between the last time I saw you and now, but you're not the Jules I knew back in Seoul. The Jules whose eyes light up the moment she sees me, or the Jules who smiles so easily."

"You're right. I'm not the same naive girl you met all those months ago. Back then, I was so gullible and stupid, but not anymore. So yeah, I suppose you don't know me," she affirmed, fixing him with a pointed stare.

"So, you're saying that what we shared back in Seoul doesn't mean anything?" he asked, his lips set in a grim line.

"You're so good with words. Why don't you tell me whether or not it was real?" she asked with a raised brow.

Noah shook his head. "What does that even mean?" He sighed again. "You know what, don't bother answering that. At least answer me this, is the baby you're carrying mine?" he stared expectantly back at her.

"I don't have to tell you anything," she replied, folding her hands over her chest.

"Jules," he said in a warning tone.

"Noah," she returned, challenging, firing up her blue eyes.

Noah looked away from her, and after another release of air, he began pacing the small space between the couch and the small coffee table. Jules watched him carefully as her heart continued to hammer against her chest.

"The fact that you refuse to answer my question only proves that you're deflecting because it's mine," he said thoughtfully.

"It doesn't prove anything," Jules retorted.

"Judging by the look of your belly, I can only assume that you're in your last trimester," he asserted, looking at her covered belly. "That would mean the baby was conceived our last time together, which also confirms that it's mine. Unless..."

Jules looked at him quizzically, waiting for him to finish his statement.

"Was there someone else?" he asked.

"Wha—" Jules stammered. She felt as if someone had just doused her in a bucket of cold water. Finding her tongue, she managed to ask, "What do you mean by if there was someone else?"

Noah looked at her pointedly. "I mean, were you seeing someone else?"

Jules widened her eyes, and her mouth formed an O, but it quickly morphed into anger. "Do I look like a two-timer to you?" she seethed.

"I don't know, you remember?" he asked, raising an eyebrow in challenge.

Jules walked up to him, anger simmering in the blue depths of her eyes. She raised her hand to his chest and used her index finger to poke him in his chest as she spoke. "I am and will never be a cheat. After seeing what my dad did to my mom, I could never be that cruel," she affirmed as an angry tear slid down her cheek.

"Jules," Noah spoke softly, reaching up to touch her. She stepped away from him, and his hand fell helplessly by his side.

"To answer your question, I have only ever been intimate with one person, and that so happened to be you. Although, I can't say the same for you, though. I am loyal, and I would have never shared such a precious gift with anyone else like it meant nothing to me." She turned her back to him as she tried to wipe away the evidence of her weakness.

"Jules, I'm sorry. I let my anger get the best of me," Noah apologized. Jules waved off his apology before turning back to him.

"As much as I now wish it weren't true, the baby is yours. Congratulations, you're about to be the father to a little girl," she clapped mockingly.

Noah stared at her wordlessly, his eyes filled with remorse.

Chapter Thirteen

The doorbell rang just as Cora descended the last step into the foyer. Walking over to the front door, she threw it open to see Noah standing on the other side.

"Good morning, Miss—I mean Cora. How are you?" he greeted with a grin.

Cora replied warmly. "Hello, Noah. I'm well, thanks. How are you? Please come in." She stepped aside, granting him access.

Noah gave her a grateful look as he stepped inside. "I'm okay. I didn't sleep much, but other than that, everything's great," he informed her.

Cora's brows shifted upward, and her forehead tightened as she gave him a look of concern. "Is it the room? Was it too cold? Was the bed too short?" she quizzed him.

"What?" Noah's eyes flickered in surprise. "No. The room was great. It was perfect," he affirmed. "I just..." his words trailed off, and he sifted his fingers through his low-cut hair. "I was just anxious for today to come," he confessed, his apprehension shining through his forest-green eyes.

Cora gave him a reassuring look and squeezed his arm lightly. "This is your first doctor's appointment. It's normal to be nervous."

A shadow of a smile dawned on his lips. "I run toward danger without hesitation, but the thought of seeing one tiny little human, someone I made on a monitor, scares me." He chuckled in disbelief.

Cora looked at him knowingly. "It happens to the best of us," she said simply. "Why don't you wait in the living room until Jules is ready?" she offered.

"Sounds great," Noah agreed, following her to the room. She watched as the young man came to a stop by the wall and folded his hands behind him, his feet slightly apart as he stood in a soldier's post. "You know the couch won't eat you," she told him, a lopsided grin playing at her lips.

Noah looked at her apologetically before settling on the couch.

"Would you like me to get you anything while you're waiting on Jules?" Cora looked expectantly at him.

"No thanks. I ate over at the Willberry Eats," he expressed.

"All right." Cora watched Noah sit perfectly still while she was fidgeting where she stood. The questions rested at the tip of her tongue, attempting to force themselves out into the open so that she could satisfy her curiosity. So far, she knew that Noah was the baby's father, he was an army man, and Jules hadn't seen or spoken to him in over seven months. The gaps in the story had put Cora on edge.

"Ahem," she attempted to clear her throat.

Noah's head snapped up in her direction.

"Why don't I go see what's holding up Jules?"

"Okay," he replied.

Cora turned and walked out of the room. As much as she wanted answers, she didn't want to break her daughter's trust as she knew from first-hand experience the consequences of doing so. She would have to exercise patience and wait for her daughter to tell her.

She knocked on her daughter's door before entering. "Jules, what's wrong?" she asked, taking in her daughter's state of undress. "Why aren't you dressed?"

Jules sighed heavily before taking a seat on the bed. Cora walked into the room further.

"Do you need some help picking out an outfit?"

Jules shook her head no.

Cora sat beside Jules. "I don't know what happened between you and Noah, but I want you to know that I'm here for you when you're ready to talk." She bumped her daughter's shoulder in a playful way.

Jules beamed at her mother. "Thanks, Mom," she replied.

Cora looked happily at Jules and put her arm around her daughter lovingly. "All right, let me see what you plan to wear," she encouraged.

"I was thinking either this one or this one." Jules lifted the two choices for Cora to see.

"That one." Cora pointed to the green sundress.

"That's what I was thinking," Jules replied with a grin. "Can you help me put it on? It has a zip in the back that I won't be able to do up," she asked.

Cora stood from the bed and helped her daughter get dressed. "There you go," she said, standing back to look at her. "You look so beautiful." She reached over to cup Jules's face affectionately. Jules placed her hand over her mother's and smiled back at her.

"Let's not keep that young man waiting any longer."

"Okay," Jules agreed. She walked her to the living room. Noah stood instantly when they walked through the door.

Cora stood off to the corner, watching the two young people move awkwardly around each other. "You two should get going. Your appointment is in half an hour," she said, ushering them to the front door. "I'll see you when you get back," she told Jules.

"See you later, Mom."

"Bye, Cora."

After closing the door, she decided to go spend some time with her mother.

"Hi," she greeted the nurse as she entered the room.

"Hi," the woman greeted back with a grin. "Your mom's awake. She's much stronger today," she advised.

"That's good to hear." Cora smiled appreciatively.

"I'll give you some privacy," the nurse said, moving away from the bed.

"Thank you. I made some cinnamon rolls earlier. They're in the kitchen if you would like one, and milk or juice is in the refrigerator."

"Thanks," the woman replied, leaving the room.

"Hi, Mom," she said as she sat in the chair by the bed. Becky's eyes hunted the room until they landed on Cora.

Cora's heart clunked to the bottom of her chest at how difficult it was for her mother to even look at her. She reached over and rested her palm over her mother's hand. "Remember the time I got chewing gum stuck in my hair? Instead of coming to you for help, I found a pair of scissors and cut out the bubblegum bits." She chuckled. "I remember the horrified look on your face." Cora shook her head. "I started crying even before you said a word. Instead of scolding me, you swept me up into your arms and kissed me on my forehead. Then you told me that you were proud of me for making tough decisions, but then you said I love you, and I felt so much better." Cora looked over at her mother to see her staring back at her. Her brown eyes swirled with so much emotion, so much more than her words could have conveyed.

"I love you so much, Mom," she expressed deeply. "I don't think I've said it enough, but I do. It's because of what you did for me that I am who I am today, why I was able to raise two incredible girls." She paused as a lump lodged in her throat and her eyes misted over. As she swallowed, trying to dislodge the lump, a single tear snuck past the barrier and slid down her cheek. Cora reached up to wipe it away. She tried to muster a smile as she turned her gaze back to her mother, but she was sure the look on her face looked more like a grimace.

"I wish we had more time," she said barely above a whisper as another tear slipped down her cheek, then another. She closed her eyes, trying to stem them, but they still managed to squeeze from the corners.

She finally reached for the hem of her blouse and lifted it, using the material to dab her eyes, soaking up the escaped moisture.

When her eyes again searched out her mother, she was alarmed to see tears running down the sides of her mother's face as she cried silently. The look of sadness and helplessness hit Cora so hard that her heart could have cracked in two. It felt as if a wrench was twisting her insides.

"Mom, please don't cry," she hurried to say, standing and using her thumb to move the moisture from her cheeks. "I just wanted you to know how much you mean to me before it's..." she trailed off. She noticed Becky's mouth tremble.

"Mmm...mmmm...mmmmmm"

"Mom, relax. Don't try to speak," Cora urged, placing a hand on the bed railing and over on her mother's chest, feeling the faint beats of her heart against her palm. Still, Becky continued to struggle to try to speak. At the distressing sound of the machine displaying her vitals, Cora froze as she looked at her mother, who seemed to be struggling to breathe.

"Mom, Mom, please stay with me," she cried in despair, reaching for the oxygen mask to put over her face.

"What happened?" the nurse who'd just burst through the door asked as she came to the bed to look at Becky.

"I...she was trying to talk...I-I-I tol-d her not to, but she kept trying an-an..." Cora released a frightening sound from her lips.

"It's okay. She's fine," the nurse assured her. "She just got a little too excited, didn't we, Becky?" the woman asked as she placed her stethoscope against Becky's chest before pressing down on the veins in her left wrist.

The nurse turned to Cora, forcing her to drag her gaze away from her mother. "I'm going to give her a sedative so she can get some rest," she informed Cora.

Cora nodded as her words failed her. The woman touched her arm reassuringly and gave her a small smile before going through the contents of the top drawer of the medical table by the bed. "All right, here we go," she said, lifting up a small vial in one hand and a syringe in the next. After measuring out the dosage, she injected it into the IV tube.

"She should be out within the next three to five minutes. If you want, you can sit with her until she falls asleep," the woman told Cora.

"Thank you," Cora replied. The nurse again left the room, and Cora held her mother's hand between hers. "You're gonna be all right," she promised her mother, but it sounded hollow even to her own ears. She sat and watched her mother's eyes slowly flutter closed. Releasing a heavy sigh, she got up and left.

Cora couldn't stay in the house, not after what happened with Becky. She needed someone to talk to. She needed her sisters.

After informing the nurse where she'd be, Cora walked through the front door and followed the path bordered by shrubs and small ornamentals toward the inn. She came up to the colonial-style great house that was now transformed into a guesthouse with all the modern amenities to provide the guests with comfortable accommodations while appealing to their desire for authentic historical experiences.

"Hi, Cora," Marg greeted her as a broad smile brightened her face.

"Hi, Marg," she returned. "Have you seen Drea?" she asked.

"I believe she took a break and went by the eatery," the woman told her.

"I'm gonna go try and catch her there. I need to discuss something with her and Jo.

"All right," Marg replied. "We'll catch up later."

Another three minutes and Cora was stepping through the doors of Willberry Eats. She immediately spotted Andrea and Jo sitting in the far corner. She made a beeline for them.

"Are you guys having a lunch date without me?" she asked with a raised brow.

"Hey, Sis," Andrea greeted her as she pulled out a chair and sat. "If we knew you were coming, we would have waited."

"I would have asked Daniel to whip up another plate of his special for you," Jo added.

"That's okay." She waved them off. "I'm not really hungry." Her sisters' faces scrunched up with confusion.

"What's wrong?" Jo asked, the same time Andrea asked, "Is something wrong with Mom?"

Cora held Andrea's eyes as she nodded solemnly. "She had an episode a little earlier...it was...scary," she informed them, staring off into space as the images of her mother in distress hit her like a ton of bricks once more.

She turned her gaze back to her sisters to see them staring back at her in alarm.

"We have to do something really memorable for Mom before she...leaves," she suggested.

The sisters nodded in agreement.

Chapter Fourteen

"Hi, Jules. It's so good to see you staying up to date with your checkups," Doctor Wright greeted her with a smile the moment she stepped into her office. "And who might this be?" she asked, looking behind Jules.

Jules didn't bother to turn around. "Um, that's Noah. The baby's father."

The doctor blinked, and her lips turned up in a wide grin. "It's a pleasure to meet you, Noah," she said, extending her hand to him.

"Thanks. It is a pleasure to meet you too." He returned her smile and shook her hand.

"I'm happy you chose to come to Jules's checkup. We're at the crucial stage of her pregnancy. She needs all the support she can get as well as the baby."

Jules blushed as the implications of her doctor's words hung heavy in the air.

"I would have been here a lot sooner, but I was deployed

for a very long time, but now that I'm back, I don't intend on going anywhere else," Noah informed her.

"Oh, you were in the army?" Dr. Wright's gaze landed on Jules, who was looking anywhere else but at her before it went back to Noah.

"Yes, ma'am," he confirmed with a slight bow.

"Thank you for your service to our country. Your sacrifice and your courage will never go unnoticed," the woman spoke appreciatively.

"Thank you. I'm honored to serve my country," Noah replied.

"All right, let's get this show on the road then. Jules, I need to speak with my receptionist. In the meantime, Noah, please help her onto the examination table," Dr. Wright spoke. "You know what to do," she finished looking at Jules, who nodded in understanding.

After the doctor left, Jules turned to the slightly raised bed. She went to lift her leg onto the elevated ledge when she felt Noah's hands at her waist, supporting her weight.

"I can make it up there on my own, you know," she said through gritted teeth.

"I know," Noah affirmed, but he didn't release her waist and proceeded to help her off the ledge until she was situated on the table.

"Thanks," she muttered, not looking at him.

"You're welcome," he returned.

She finally looked up to find his green eyes already on her. Her heart skipped a beat at what she saw in them, and she quickly looked away. "Could you turn around...please? I need to settle myself and fix my clothes before the doctor gets back."

Wordlessly, Noah turned his back to her, and Jules fixed herself until only her naked belly was in view.

"You can turn back around," she informed Noah.

Noah's eyes instantly found her belly, and his eyes widened

as his lips parted before he shut it with a smack and his gaze shuttered.

"Okay. Are we ready?" the doctor asked as she stepped back into the room.

Jules nodded.

Noah took place on the opposite side of the table as the doctor sidled up to it on the other side. She squirted the gel onto Jules's belly, causing an involuntary shiver from Jules. She switched on the monitor and reached for the probe, placing it on Jules's tummy. Soon the screen was displaying a black-and-white image of Jules's uterus and her baby girl tucked to one side with her finger in her mouth.

"Well, Noah, say hello to your daughter," the doctor said, glancing over the bed at him.

Jules's eyes followed her path. Noah stood still like a statue, his eyes wide with wonder. As the realization of what he was seeing dawned on him, his lips crept slowly upward until he was full-out smiling.

"I'm going to be a father," he spoke reverently. His gaze averted to Jules, and she could already see the love that he had for their daughter reflected in their depths. "I'm going to be a father," he repeated, holding her gaze, waiting. Jules gestured approvingly.

"She looks just as healthy as your last visit, Jules. That's good," the doctor said in a pleased tone. She looked up at Noah, who was staring at the monitor. "You should talk to her and see how well she responds to your voice," she instructed.

Noah looked at the doctor with apprehension before his gaze switched to Jules. Jules subtly gestured her approval. There was no way she could deprive him of getting this precious time with their daughter. After all, she'd deprived him for so long. A wave of guilt passed through her. Regardless of their current relationship, she realized now it wasn't fair for her to have kept his child from him.

Bittersweet Memories

"Hi, sweetie...it's me, your father, Noah."

At the sound of his voice, the baby began to stir in her belly, and Jules could feel the small fluttering as she became active. Her head fell on her chest as she watched Noah crouch at her tummy, the look of awe plastered on his face.

"Keep going," the doctor encouraged.

"I know I haven't been here, and you're just getting to know my voice, but I can assure you, you will hear it every day from this day until you're born because I am never leaving."

"There she goes," the doctor highlighted on the screen as the baby quickly moved from the side she had been resting on to the other side. Her tiny feet thumped against Jules's belly, making tiny prints against her skin.

"Beautiful," Noah breathed out lovingly as he watched the action on the monitor before settling his eyes on her belly.

"You can touch it," she offered.

Noah's face registered surprise as his eyes snapped to her before moving down to her belly. He tentatively reached out his hand and rested his palm on her belly. Instantaneously, the baby let out a wild kick that reverberated against his palm.

"This is amazing," he beamed ear to ear. Again, his eyes sought out Jules, and she became trapped in them. "Thank you for this gift."

Jules was left speechless by his gratitude.

"Okay. Like I said before, everything seems fine," Dr. Wright reiterated, pulling them out of whatever trance they had been in. "I'm still monitoring your fluids, but everything is normal so far. I'm gonna get the sonogram. I'll be back."

Jules nodded, grateful. After fixing her clothes, she sat up and threw her legs over the edge of the table. "Did you mean what you said earlier? That you'll be here for the baby's birth, I mean?"

Noah turned to look at her seriously. "I did," he confirmed.

"That's why I booked the room at your family's inn for the next two months."

"I didn't know that," she gave out, surprised.

"I want to be here, Jules. I want to be as much a part of my baby's life as I can." Noah ran his fingers through his short hair. Jules's attention was drawn to the action, and her fingers twitched. Noah paced the small space, his hands coming up to lock across his chest. Jules watched in confusion. Suddenly, he came to a stop and faced her.

"I don't know what it is that I've done to you for you to be treating me the way you have."

Jules snickered disbelievingly.

Noah ignored her outburst as he continued.

"I am a man of honor..."

She fought the urge not to roll her eyes as her anger built.

"I have always been forthright with you, but..." Noah shook his head.

"I will be here for my baby, regardless of what happens between us."

"And what does your fiancée have to say about that?" she asked, folding her hands atop her belly and fixing him with a pointed stare.

"What?" Noah's eyebrows jogged up his forehead. "What are you talking about?"

Jules's eyes narrowed to slits, and her mouth set in a grim line. She opened her mouth to blast him, but...

"Okay, here we go." The doctor stepped into the room, halting her words. The grin on her face froze as she looked at the two young adults with their hands folded across their chests, tension permeating the room. "Did I miss something?" she asked.

"No. It's fine," Noah recovered first, offering the woman a reassuring smile. He collected the sonogram from the doctor, who was still staring between them skeptically.

Jules got down from the table and walked through the door that Noah held open for her with her back as stiff as she could manage.

"Thanks again, Dr. Wright." Jules managed to put a smile on her face, albeit a strained one.

The two parents made their way to the vehicle, neither of them exchanging a word, but as Noah pulled out of the parking lot onto the highway, he looked over at Jules before turning his attention back to the road. This he did a number of times which only served to irritate Jules more than she already was.

"What!" she exploded.

Noah turned his attention back to the road without a word. After more than a minute, he finally asked, "Why do you think I have a fiancée?"

Jules turned her neck in his direction before turning to face forward. "It doesn't matter." She shrugged.

"Obviously, it does," Noah refuted. "Even worse...it's a lie."

Jules's head snapped to him again, and she narrowed her eyes in suspicion. "You're telling me that you don't have a fiancée back in South Carolina?" she asked, staring at him, examining him.

"I don't know where you got your intel, but and I repeat, I Do Not Have A Fiancée. Not back home, not anywhere on the planet," he said seriously.

"Who's Dina?" she asked.

Noah's knuckles tightened on the steering wheel until they were almost pale. "Where did you hear that name?" he asked, his voice strained.

Jules looked at the man beside her with newfound contempt. She turned her head and looked straight ahead, unable to look at him anymore.

"I called your parents...back in Seoul when I found out I was pregnant. A woman answered the phone that wasn't your mother. Oh, but she was very eager to let me know that she was your fiancée, you know...Do you know how humiliated I felt?" An angry tear slipped down her cheek. "I felt like a fool believing that you were my knight in shining armor when you were, in fact, using me. I won't make that mistake again." She used the end of the sweater she had on over her dress to wipe away the wetness from her face.

She heard Noah release a heavy breath beside her. "Jules, I'm sorry that happened to you, but I need you to believe me that none of what that woman told you is true," he implored.

"So, you don't know her?" she asked.

"I do." Noah sighed. "She's my ex-girlfriend."

Jules's heart thumped against her chest, and her eyes widened in surprise, but she quickly shuttered them, not wanting to believe a word he said.

"On my first deployment, I had planned to marry her. I got the ring and everything, but when I came back, she confessed that she had cheated on me with my best friend. Turned out they'd been sneaking around behind my back throughout the whole time I was away. I broke up with her on the spot."

Jules's conscience pricked at her, and she glanced over at the man in remorse and sympathy.

"I'm sorry that happened to you."

Noah nodded in acknowledgment. "When I met you, I'd already been broken up with Dina for over a year. I should have told you about her, and if I had known it would have come back to bite me in the butt, I would have told you."

"But why was she at your parent's home?" she asked, needing to get everything out.

"Her parents and my parents are friends. They're very close, actually, and my parents treat her like a daughter," he explained. "She's been trying to get me back, but I'll never take her back," he affirmed.

Jules felt a sense of relief that none of it was true. However...

"Do you still love her?"

Noah looked on contemplatively.

"I will always love her because she was my first love, but I am not in love with her," he explained.

Jules nodded in understanding again, but she wasn't sure she was satisfied with the answer.

Chapter Fifteen

"Where are you taking me?"

"It's a surprise. Remember?"

"Can't I have just one guess? Or maybe a little peak?" Jules reached up, attempting to pull the blindfold from her face.

"Not a fat chance," Noah replied, catching her hand before it could remove the cloth. He intertwined their fingers as he led her down a flight of stairs. The sun's rays pelting her skin indicated that they were still outdoors.

"Noah, we were on a train for two and a half hours. Is there nothing you can give me for exhibiting such patience?" she asked.

"What I will tell you is that we are about ten minutes away."

"You better not be lying," she warned, earning a chuckle from him.

"I'm not lying. Do you trust me?" he asked.

Jules didn't have to think about her answer. "I do."

"Good."

Less than a minute after, Jules could hear the rhythmic sound of waves moving back and forth somewhere in the distance, and she could smell the salt of the ocean carried with the breeze as it caressed her skin and filled her nostrils. "Oh my gosh, I know where you're taking me," she cheesed.

Noah laughed. "Let's not ruin the surprise until we get there," he cautioned.

Jules made the motion of zipping her lips, earning another chuckle from him. Her own face broke out in a wide smile as she anticipated the surprise.

Soon, her slipper-clad feet sank with each step she took forward as the sand became displaced around them. The sound of the waves lapping at the shore was even louder now, and she could hear the sound of a few seagulls in the distance.

"We're here." Jules's body vibrated with excitement. Slowly, Noah released her from the blindfold. Jules blinked a few times, trying to adjust to the sudden brightness around her. A surprised gasp left her lips, and she quickly spun around to Noah, who was already watching her.

"This is...wow."

"I never thought I could have made you speechless," Noah snickered, bringing her into the cocoon of his arms.

"You continue to surprise me like this, and you are in for a lot more speechless moments," she promised, staring up into his green eyes. Noah dipped his head until their lips met, and they shared a sweet kiss. When he released her, Jules turned back to the spectacular view before her. The pristine blue waters stared back at her, beckoning for her to come to enjoy it. The sand was the whitest she'd ever seen and shone brightly by the reflection of the light.

"When did you get time to plan this?" she asked, walking over to the single picnic table adorned with a magnificent spread for them

"I have a friend," he told her as her arms came up to wrap

around his neck. No music was needed as they rocked from side to side. Jules rested her head on his chest, listening to the steady beating of his heart. Her eyes fluttered shut.

"Noah..."

"Hmm?"

"*I love y...*" *Her eyes flew open in alarm as realization hit her that she had almost made a slip. She felt Noah go still.* "*I love spending time with you,*" *she hurriedly called out.*

Noah pulled back to look at her with a tight grin and searching eyes.

"What?" *She laughed.*

"*I love spending time with you. It makes me want to do things like this for you.*"

Warmth crept up the sides of her neck to her cheeks as she blushed. Relief settled in her chest that he hadn't picked up on her blunder.

Jules shook out of her reverie and sighed. She couldn't believe she'd come so close to telling Noah that she loved him all those months back. She really had been naive. Back then, her feelings had been strong for the man. Given the right conditions, she would have shouted it from the mountain tops, but in the past seven months of being alone and jaded by his perceived betrayal, she was warier than ever. However, she couldn't deny that the past few days had reminded her so much of his caring side, of how readily he was willing to do things that made her comfortable. She remembered having a craving for blueberry cheesecake muffins from her cousin Kerry's bakery and that he'd left to pick them up for her. Then she craved a double fudge sundae drizzled with caramel and pecans. He'd dropped what he was doing and drove her to the ice cream shop in the town. She had to admit that it would be easy to fall back into the routine they'd had back in Seoul.

Her mother had invited him almost every evening to have dinner with them, and although, for the most part, he had declined the invites, he had chosen to attend the past three and had met quite a few of her family. They all seemed to like him very much. A smile graced her lips as she thought about it. As quickly as it came, it went. She wasn't sure what it was that Noah wanted, and she didn't want to get her hopes up only for them to be dashed against the rock. Maybe it was pregnancy hormones building up her hopes.

Throwing a sweater over her shoulders, she made her way to the back door to have a seat on the wraparound porch. The snow had all melted, but the time was still chilly. She welcomed the sun that was raining down its warmth and breaking up the monochrome of drabness.

As she sat looking out at the water, contemplating her next move, her phone rang. Jules reached for the small device bringing it to eye level. Her brows furrowed at the unfamiliar area code. Tentatively she brought the phone to her ear.

"Hello?"

"Hi, sweetheart."

Jules's mood immediately soured, and her lips stretched into a thin line.

"Why are you calling me, Dad?"

"Wow, that was harsh." The man chuckled.

Jules felt her eyebrows ride up to her hairline. "I'm hanging up," she threatened.

"Please don't do that," Joel rushed out. "Just give me a chance," he pleaded.

Jules rolled her eyes as she released a huff of air. "You have five minutes," she advised him.

"Thank you," he responded gratefully.

There was a long pause as she waited for him to say what he wanted. "Time's wasting, Dad," she reminded him.

"How are you?" he asked after a few more seconds.

"I'm fine," she answered in a clipped tone.

"How's your sister?"

Jules moved the phone from her ear and stared at it for a while before putting it back to her ear.

"You're asking me about Erin? Why don't you pick up the phone and call her? She has a number, you know."

"You're right. I'm sorry. It's just that she doesn't pick up when I call," Joel explained.

"That makes two of us," she muttered.

"What do you mean?"

"It doesn't matter." She released an exasperated breath. "Look, Dad, your time's running out. Could you get to the point of this call?" She knew she was being rude to her father, but quite frankly, she didn't care, especially after what he put their family through.

"I spoke to your mother a few months back..." Jules sat up straighter in the chair. "She told me you were pregnant."

"And you're just now calling me?" she asked in a disbelieving tone.

"I know I should have called sooner, but...I wanted to give you space. I didn't want to upset you."

"Yeah, well then, you shouldn't have called me at all," she threw back at him.

"Jules, I am really sorry for what I did to your mother and to you girls. It was unconscionable, and I didn't think—"

"Think what? That you would have been caught?" she bit out angrily.

"I never meant to hurt you, Jules...any of you," Joel pleaded.

"Yeah, well, you did, Dad. You should have thought of the consequences before you broke your vows to Mom and before you shattered our trust." Her chest tightened. "Look, Dad. I can't do this. I have to go."

"Sweetheart, wait," he begged.

"I'm sorry. I can't talk to you right now." With that, Jules disconnected the call.

Bittersweet Memories

She sat staring out at the tranquil water as she muffled the sobs with her fist in her mouth. The tears cascaded down her cheeks and dripped from her chin. Her father's betrayal, although more than a year ago, still hurt like a fresh wound. Whenever she thought of his callousness, it would bring her to tears.

How could someone who claimed to love you betray your trust? She still loved her father, and she did miss him, but she wasn't at the place to want to have a relationship with him because she was still mad at him for what he did. Her thoughts switched to the fact that she'd almost become the other woman because of Noah's ex. She'd felt used, but mostly she had been ashamed— ashamed that she had become the other woman, living out her worst fears. She felt as if she'd been put in the blender and ground out like fine powder.

Her mind flashed to Erin, wondering what she'd been up to and if she knew that their father had been trying to reach her. She wondered if Erin was deliberately ignoring his calls. She knew it had been rough for Erin to find out about their father. Erin had been distant and thoughtless. Though she was mad that her sister was blowing her off, along with everyone else, she couldn't help but think this was all because of her father's betrayal. It was obvious that Erin was keeping something from the family, and she bet it was something that had caused her to break up with her boyfriend of over five years. This definitely wasn't the Erin who would give up her right lung and give up the other if it came to that, just to protect her little sister. This Erin was different— cold and distant.

"Penny, for your thoughts?"

Jules turned her head to the side to see her mother staring back at her in concern. She turned back and looked out at the harbor. "Dad called me."

"Oh," came her mother's surprised response. "What did he say?"

Jules didn't answer the question. Instead, she inclined her head to look at her mother and asked, "Are you guys talking again?"

Cora breathed in deeply before releasing it. She walked over to the porch railing and leaned against it as she stared at her daughter. "We're not friends, but I am trying to forgive him for what he did," she explained.

"Is that why you told him I'm pregnant?" Jules asked seriously.

"He's your father, Jules. Regardless of what he did, he will always be your father. Although our relationship didn't work out, there is no doubt that he loves you and your sister more than anything in the world," Cora replied, staring at her daughter compassionately.

Jules looked away from her mother, her brows furrowing and a scowl framing her lips.

"Give him a chance to make it up to you, Jules. Let him be the father that you need, sweetie," Cora implored.

"Why are you pushing this?" Jules asked defensively.

Cora looked at her daughter, her blue-gray eyes filled with emotions. "I don't want you to live with any regrets. I spent more than two decades not talking to my dad, and in the end, I wish I had time to spend with him to make up for the lost time, but I was too late, and I was filled with so many regrets." Cora's lips turned down, and her eyes closed briefly. When they opened, Jules could see the sadness etched in them.

"I don't want you to live a life of regret, sweetie. I know it'll be hard, but you need to forgive your father before it is too late."

Jule's eyes widened in alarm.

"Is Dad...Is he dying?" she asked feebly.

Chapter Sixteen

Valentine's Day

Jules's ears perked up at the sound of car tires crunching against snow-covered gravel. Putting down the bowl of red- and white-colored popcorn she'd been stringing on the nylon cord, she slowly raised herself from the couch and walked toward the large French window in the living room. Pulling back the heavy curtain, she peered through the transparent glass. Several cars were currently lining up along the designated parking spot.

"They're here!" Her voice carried to the kitchen where her mother and aunts were busy preparing food for the Valentine's Day family cookout. She walked out into the hallway to see Aunt Jo a few meters ahead of her as she made her way toward the foyer and the front door. She continued after her.

"Hey, kiddo. How's my favorite niece?" Uncle Luke greeted as he stepped through the door, Aunt Maria and Aunt

Stacey coming in behind him. He swept Jo up in his arms, completely dwarfing her with his large frame. Jules remained by the stairs, watching their interaction.

"You say that to all your nieces." Jo chuckled as she tilted her head back to look at him.

"That's because you all have a special place in my heart," Uncle Luke rallied with a wide grin.

"Good save," Jo snickered, earning laughs from the others. "I'm glad you guys could make it, short notice and all."

"Are you kidding me? We wouldn't miss it for the world," Uncle Luke responded, finally setting Jo back on her feet. He beamed down at her. Laugh lines framed his mouth, and the corners of his eyes crinkled.

"Hi, Aunt Maria," Jo turned to greet the short woman beside him. She leaned over and placed a kiss on the woman's cheek, then turned to Aunt Stacy. She bent lower and placed a kiss against the older woman's cheek. "I'm glad you were able to come today, Aunt Stacy."

"There's no way I would turn down a well-cooked meal and the best company money can't buy," she quipped with a toothy smile.

"That's true," Jo agreed, and the others shook their heads in agreement. A brief moment of silence passed around them.

"I'm going to visit with Becky if you don't mind," Aunt Stacy spoke up. The others inclined their heads in acknowledgment and watched her motorized scooter roll across the foyer.

"Hi, Aunt Stacy," Jules greeted the woman as she came close to where she stood.

"Hi, dear," her great-aunt said kindly. Her eyes went to Jules's belly. "How's the little one?" she asked.

A grin played on Jules's lip. "She's fine. Although she is kicking a whole lot more, and I live in the bathroom now," she informed the old woman.

"That's a good thing, or else you'd be wondering if something's wrong, be happy," the woman advised.

Jules inclined her head in acceptance.

"I'm headed to visit Becky."

Jules nodded, moving closer to the steps to give her wheelchair enough space to pass. She turned to see Uncle Luke and Aunt Maria headed her way.

"Hi, sweetheart," Uncle Luke said. Jules smiled in greeting as he enveloped her as he had Jo.

"Oh, you're glowing," Aunt Maria observed when he set her back on her feet.

"Thanks," she replied. They left her and headed for the kitchen just as Kerry came through the door with her daughter Amy.

"You're here, good. Now I can go help Daniel at the eatery," Jo said, relieved, bringing her cousin in for a short hug. "Hi, Amy. It's so good to see you again," she greeted the young woman.

The young woman smiled before replying with "Hi," and a shy wave.

"Are you sure you and Daniel aren't cutting out to have some early Valentine's fun without us?" Kerry asked with a suggestive raise of her brow.

Jo playfully hit her cousin on her shoulder. "We have to prepare for the lunch crowd so that we can make it back here for the cookout," she explained.

"I know. I was just playing with you." Kerry chuckled.

"So, is Ethan coming?" Jo asked.

"Yeah. He said he'd be here soon. He just had to go into the office to take care of a few things," Kerry replied.

"Okay. I'll see you guys in a bit," Jo said and left.

"Hi, Jules. How are you?" Kerry asked as she headed in her direction.

"Hi, I'm fine," she responded with a smile of her own.

Kerry nodded before turning to her daughter. "Amy, you remember Cora's daughter, right?"

"Yes, I do," Amy replied.

"I'm gonna go help the others in the kitchen. You two should get to know each other better," Kerry suggested. "Sophia and Emma will be here a bit later." Kerry headed for the kitchen, leaving them alone.

Jules turned to her cousin in warm greeting. It was uncanny how much Amy looked like her mother. She had the same blond hair, light brown eyes, and an angular face. If Jules had to guess, she would say they were about the same height and had the same body type. It was like looking in the mirror of time at a young Kerry. "I'm stringing popcorn for the cookout if you'd like to help," she offered.

"Yeah. I'd love that," Amy accepted with a grateful smile.

The two young women walked down the hall toward the living room. They spent the next half hour stringing popcorn and talking. So far, Jules learned that Amy was studying to become a cardiologist, her favorite hobbies were chess and tennis, and that she hadn't had much time for friends and dating because she was so focused on finishing school.

"I have to stay focused; I have to keep on my A game, so I really can't afford any type of distraction, especially from guys," Amy expressed.

Jules's hand instinctively touched her belly as a thought ran through her mind. She quickly squashed the thought and changed the conversation to talking about what they each loved about the small coastal town.

More family members arrived within the hour. Jules and Amy brought their popcorn chains out to the patio, and Uncle Luke and the other men present assisted them in tying them on the posts of the pergola and the railings of the back porch, along with heart-shaped decorations made out of cartridge paper. Vases of faux red roses and blush pink peonies decorated the long concrete table and the three additional wooden tables they'd taken from the storehouse.

"You guys went all out with this." Jules turned to her mother with an impressed look.

Cora gave her a small smile. "We want to make as many memories as we can for the next little while that we have with Mom."

Jules's nodded in understanding. She tried to smile, but her lips only went up a fraction before flattening as emotions welled her throat shut. It was hard for her to imagine that soon, her grandmother would no longer be around.

Cora reached out to rub her arm comfortingly. "I invited Noah," she said after some time of them standing in silence.

Jules's eyes snapped to her mother in surprise. "You did?"

"I did," Cora confirmed. "Although, I think you should have done it yourself," she continued, giving her daughter a sober look. "You're having a child with him, Jules. That makes him a part of this family. I still don't know what happened between you two, and I promised I wouldn't push, but I need you to understand that this little girl you're about to bring into this world has to come first. So, whether or not you two get back together, you have to find a way to get along."

"Okay," Jules replied, her eyes downcast. "You're right."

"Good, because he's here."

Her head shot up, and she turned to see Noah making his way toward them.

"I'm gonna go get Mom," Cora said before walking off. She stopped to greet Noah and then continued toward the house.

Noah walked toward Jules, stopping less than a foot away from her. "Hi," he greeted, his hands burrowing into his pockets as he watched her carefully.

"Hi," Jules replied. Her voice was barely above a whisper.

"So, this is nice." His head turned to the side to quickly survey the activities before looking back at her.

"Yeah," Jules agreed with a slight nod. "My family will find any excuse to have a cookout. I bet if they didn't have to work, they'd be here day in and day out firing up the grill and eating hot dogs and chips, and Uncle Luke would probably be challenging everyone to try beating him at poker." Jules's shoulders pulled up to her ear as she shook in mock horror.

Noah chuckled. "Sounds a lot like my family. They love these sorts of things."

The light, melodious sound of his laughter was infectious, and Jules found her lips turning up in a wide grin as she watched him talk. The twinkle in his eyes drew her in.

"Anything to be together," he said after a short pause. Jules noted the faraway look in his green eyes.

"You miss them," she stated rather than asked.

Noah blinked twice before his eyes settled on her knowing ones. His lips caved in on each other before opening to reply, "I do."

"And you haven't been home since your deployment?" This time she asked.

"I haven't." He breathed in deeply before releasing it and turned to look out at the landscape leading toward the dock. Jules waited for him to continue. "I stopped off in Seoul because I wanted to see you before I headed to South Carolina, but..."

"You found out I was pregnant and skipped town," she finished for him.

Noah inclined his head to the side to look at her. "Yeah," he replied simply.

Jules gave him an apologetic look before turning and looking up at the few fluffy white clouds idly floating across the clear, blue sky.

"Can we go for a walk?"

She looked over at Noah, who was already staring back at her expectantly. "Okay," she agreed.

Jules led the way across the grass toward the cobbled stone path that ran toward her grandmother's rose garden. The noisy chatter and laughter from her family slowly dissipated as they made it to the turn leading up to the wooden gates under a beautifully arched arbor decorated by the vines of creepers coiled around its wooden exterior. By early spring, there would be a burst of color from the blooming flowers.

Noah stepped ahead of Jules and pushed the gates open before allowing her to walk ahead of him.

"This place is spectacular," she heard him say. She turned to see him admiring the flowers not affected by the season, considering it was still above ten degrees, their colorful blooms keeping the garden picturesque and fragrant.

"You should see it in late spring, back to autumn when the roses and the orchids join the party. You'd be in for a real treat then," Jules replied, smiling.

"I would love to see it. It'd be great to photograph." They continued along the path, his fingertips grazing over the flower petals along the way.

"Those are called February Gold. They're the first set of daffodils to bloom this month," Jules explained when she noticed Noah had stopped to inspect the deep yellow trumpet flowers rising from a bed of symmetrical outer petals in a lighter shade of yellow and seemingly floating on a sea of green stems.

"I like the color," he responded, snapping off a flower. Jules watched him carefully as he moved toward her. He raised the flower toward her face. Her chest rose as she gulped air into her lungs, just as he secured the flower by her ear and moved a few strands of her blond hair back. Her chest caved slowly as she stared wide-eyed at him.

His hand fell to his side, and a soft smile touched his lips and brightened his eyes. "Beautiful."

Jules lowered her gaze as her cheeks warmed over. Her

heart beat wildly as she processed his words and actions. It didn't help that she could still feel his gaze on her.

"Did you know that daffodils are poisonous to humans, especially if ingested?" she raised her head to ask as she tried to calm her frazzled nerves.

"I did not know that." Noah shook his head and laughed.

Jules couldn't contain the grin that graced her lips, and immediately her mother's words popped into her thoughts. She knew Cora was right. Jules had to give Noah a break. After all, he was going to be the father to her child.

Chapter Seventeen

"My grandfather started this garden for my grandmother a long time ago. Every year on her birthday, he presented her with a rare rose bush that he'd planted the season before. It didn't matter where in the world he had to source them from or the cost."

"Your grandfather sounds like a good man," Noah marveled as they settled on a stone bench closer to the back of the garden.

Jules beamed wryly as she looked over at him. "He and my mom didn't talk for more than twenty-five years," she revealed. "My aunts Andrea and Jo are a few years shy of that, but still, they never had a relationship with him. I didn't get to have one with him either." Jules turned to look out at the expanse of the garden, her grandfather's gift to his wife. It was undisputable that he had loved Becky very much, and there were a whole lot of the townspeople who spoke very highly of him but... "I can't tell you how good of a man he was because I didn't know him that well."

"I'm sorry."

Her head turned in his direction. Noah stared back at her with empathy in his eyes.

"It's fine," she assured him with the tilting up of her lips.

"My mom and aunts have spoken a lot about how good he had been to them when they were growing up, so I kind of got a glimpse into who he was back then. The actual fallout happened because they all wanted to leave Oak Harbor to follow their dreams, and he wanted them to stay and take over the inn. It's funny that it took his death for them all to come running back to do exactly what they had vowed not to do." She laughed at the irony.

"Death can change a person's perspective and priorities overnight," Noah added with a thoughtful look.

"You sound like you're talking from experience," Jules surmised.

Noah grinned thinly, and his eyes skirted away from her. "I lost my grandad two years ago."

"Oh, Noah. I'm so sorry," Jules spoke with heartfelt sincerity.

He didn't respond for some time. Jules noticed how his hands clenched and unclenched, the veins in his arms bulging and flattening from the tension. The action caused the muscles of her own heart to clench and unclench at the distress she felt for his pain. She had picked up that it was a hard topic for him and could only conclude that he and his granddad had been so close that the pain of losing him was still fresh to him."

"We can talk about something else if you'd like," she suggested, trying to ease his discomfort.

"No. It's fine," Noah assured her, a small smile gracing his lips to further assuage her worry.

"My granddad and I were very close...I looked up to him, and I tried my best to make him proud of me." His lips curled outward dejectedly. "There was one thing we didn't see eye to eye on." Noah gulped loudly, his Adam's Apple bobbing up and down. He leaned forward and stared at the ground.

Jules wanted to rest her hand on his arm in support. She clasped her hands in her lap instead.

After a length of silence, Noah finally spoke again. "I had a plan— join the army, then a few years after, settle down, and get married. I just didn't want it to be in South Carolina. Granddad said it was a stupid idea to pick up and leave the only home I've ever known to start life somewhere where I didn't have the protection of my family." Noah shook his head, releasing a low, heavy sigh. "I didn't see it that way. We had a huge argument before my first deployment. I said some things I'm not very proud of, and my ego didn't allow me to apologize for it before I left for duty."

Noah straightened up on the bench. He shook his head a few times.

Jules watched him...waiting.

"Two months later, I got a video call from my mom and dad telling me that he'd suffered a stroke and wanted to see me, but I wasn't allowed to leave. Two days later, the commanding officer called me into his tent to tell me that grandad had passed."

Jules noticed the moisture at the corner of his eye before a single tear slipped down his cheek. This time she reached up and placed a hand on his shoulder. Noah turned to her, his watery eyes glistening with gratitude.

"He left me his house and over six hundred acres of land."

Jules's eyes bugged out of her head, and her draw dropped down. "Six...six hundred acres?" she repeated.

Noah inclined his head to confirm that she had heard correctly.

"Wow," was all she could manage after that.

"I think that was my exact reaction when I heard it the first time too." Noah gave a short chuckle before sobering up. "I didn't get to honor him the way I wanted when he was alive, but I vowed to change that."

Jules wondered what he meant by that.

"All right, I think we've exhausted the topic of dead relatives for one day. Let's talk about something else."

Jules looked over at him to see that he was already looking at her, his green eyes unreadable. "What do you want to talk about?" she asked.

Noah's eyes descended to her bump before coming up to meet her eyes once more. Jules's brows drew together as she eyed him back.

"Have you thought about what you're going to do after the baby's born," he asked after a few seconds.

The question caught Jules by surprise. Her mouth opened, but no words came out. It wasn't that she hadn't thought about it, but the truth was she still wasn't sure, and so she had pushed it to the back of her mind.

"I don't know...yet," she finally answered, looking ahead of her. There was silence for a few more minutes. "I guess I'm just waiting to see how things go. I do want to go back to school and finish my degree, though."

"Okay," Noah replied.

"Maybe I'll enroll at the local college or Seattle," she said thoughtfully.

"What about the baby?" Noah asked.

Jules inclined her head to look questioningly at him. "What do you mean?"

"I mean, who's going to look after her while you're at school?"

She hadn't thought about that. "I could ask my mom."

"And what if she says she can't?" he pressed.

Her eyes tightened at the corners as she stared at him. "I know my mom. She wants to be a part of this baby's life as much as she can. She won't mind staying with her. Why are you asking me so many questions anyway?" she said the last part testily.

It was Noah's turn to look away. "I'm just making sure that you're thinking realistically. Our daughter will be here soon—"

"And?" she interrupted, as her skin prickled with annoyance. It felt as if whatever he was alluding to, she would have to be prepared to defend herself and the choices she made.

Noah released a heavy breath before staring at her cautiously. "I'm just saying this is a highly stressful situation, and with your grandmother needing round-the-clock care, maybe your mother won't be as available as you'd want her to be."

Jules felt her pressure rise. She folded her hands above her belly as she stared pointedly at him. "Why don't you cut to the chase and say exactly what it is that you want to say?"

Noah squared his shoulders as he sat up straighter and looked at her seriously. "I want you to move to South Carolina."

Jules felt her eyebrows jog up to her hairline. "What?" she asked, barely above a whisper.

"My parents will take care of you like you're their own. You won't need anything, and you won't have to worry about the baby while you go back to school. I think it'll ease some of the stress for you," Noah rushed out, his voice imploring her to understand.

Jules looked at him for a long time without saying anything. It seemed to her that he'd put a lot of thought into it. That was one thing she'd liked about Noah. Unlike her, he was a planner. But in this instance, all his reasonings about why moving across the country was the best option only irritated her. She looked away from him at the freshly pruned rose bushes, void of buds that would come alive again with a colorful variety of blooms in late spring. She wanted to be here to see them.

"No."

"Jules," Noah breathed out tiredly.

"I am not going to South Carolina, Noah, and that is final," she spoke strongly, turning to look at him with determination in her blue eyes. "I want to stay close to my family. As you said, my grandmother is sick, and I don't know how long she has left. I want to spend as much time as she has left by her side. Most importantly, I need my mother."

"Jules...please. Could you...can you at least take some time to think about it?" he pleaded.

"I don't have to," Jules said with a shake of her head. "My answer will still be the same two days, a month, a year from now. I need my family, Noah."

"And what about me? What am I supposed to do, Jules?" Noah asked in a low grumble.

She didn't answer immediately. Instead, her right hand ran over her stomach to rub her distended flesh soothingly as the baby started to become restless.

"I know you want to go home, and I won't stop you, but I can't go with you either. When the baby is born, we can work out an agreement for visitation when she's older," she suggested.

"This is not how I expected this to turn out." Noah sighed, sounding defeated.

Jules gave him a look of apology. "Can we get back to the cookout? I'm sure they're getting ready to send a search party for us."

Noah rose to his feet without a word. He held out his hand and helped her to her feet. They returned to the cookout in silence. Jules's mind was far from the festivities, but she plastered a smile on her lips as she approached the gathering.

"I was just about to come looking for you guys," Cora said. Jules looked over at Noah, who gave her a tight smile.

"Would you excuse me? I need to make a call."

"All right, sweetheart," Cora replied.

Jules watched Noah retreat with a mixture of angst and disappointment.

"Everything okay?" her mother asked.

Her eyes cut from him to look at Cora. "Yup."

Cora didn't look convinced, but she didn't pry.

"I'm going to say hi to Grandma," Jules said. Cora nodded and watched her walk toward Becky, who was strapped down in the specialized wheelchair they'd gotten for her.

Becky's eyes blinked in recognition, and her lips slightly turned up at Jules's approach.

"Hi, Grams," she greeted.

"I'm gonna go see if they need my help in the kitchen," Aunt Maria, who was sitting beside her, said, getting up and heading for the house.

She pulled her plastic chair closer, sat, and turned to the woman who was already looking at her. Though she couldn't talk, Jules felt as if her light brown eyes were encouraging her to tell her what was wrong.

"Noah asked me to move to South Carolina with him and his parents, and I said no." She looked down at her hands and sighed.

"He was very disappointed, but...I don't think I could go there even if I wanted to. There's just too much history between us, and I don't even know what we are right now." She released a heavy breath, and her shoulders sagged. "I told him he was free to leave and go back to South Carolina. A part of me is scared that he's going to leave, but another part is scared he won't. His being here is confusing me so much, and I don't know what to do."

Jules looked over at Becky to see her staring back at her with understanding.

Chapter Eighteen

"You're distracted."

Cora's lashes fluttered upward as her eyes settled on the obsidian ones staring back at her from across the table. "I'm sorry. What did you say?"

Jamie stared at her for a beat, his expression unreadable. "Why won't you talk to me?"

Cora blinked rapidly, and her lips parted. No words came out.

Jamie leaned forward and reached for her hand that she hadn't noticed was resting on the table. His palm was warm, and the gentle squeeze sent a tingle up her arm. She looked from their enclosed hands to his face. "I want to be there for you, Cora, but you have to let me in," he spoke softly.

"I'm sorry. It's been...hard." Cora's lips went up into a half smile, and her eyes shone with an apology. "I know it's not an excuse, but I am trying. It's just..." Her gaze darted around the room as she took in the stares of affection that the other couples surrounding them were sharing.

"I understand. I'm not trying to push you to do what you're

not ready for, but...you've been zoning out on me, on us, for a while now, and I'm worried that I'm not doing a good job of being the shoulder you can lean on. I want to be your rock, Cora." Jamie lifted their clasped hands and placed a tender kiss on the back of her hand. His dark eyes stared lovingly back at her.

Cora felt her heart constrict with guilt. Jamie was right. She was shutting him out. She'd had so much practice with handling things on her own that it almost seemed like a foreign thing to show him just how vulnerable she was. With Joel, she had always had to manage her problems and emotional well-being by herself while being not just a wife but a mother and a career woman.

It had been hard, but she'd learned to manage it, and now it was hard to let someone be there for her.

Jamie had brought her to one of the most sought-after restaurants in Seattle— the one you had to wait months to get reservations for. It had been a part of his Valentine's Day surprise to her, and yet here she was, distracted by what was happening in her family.

"There's something that I need to ask you."

Her head snapped up to stare at Jamie. Her eyes widened as she saw his free hand move to his pocket. She felt the air rush out of her lungs, and her heart pounded wildly. Was he about to ask what she thought he was?

"I know the timing might be a bit off, but..."

"Your dessert," their waiter announced, interrupting whatever it was Jamie was about to ask. They both looked up at the young man as he placed a plate with tiramisu ice cream cake before each of them.

"Thank you." Cora smiled appreciatively. The young man bowed his head in acknowledgment.

"I'll leave you two to enjoy the rest of your evening." He tipped his head before turning and leaving.

Cora looked over at Jamie to see a pensive look on his face. She opened her mouth to ask him what he wanted to ask her, but cheers and applause caught her attention. She looked over her shoulder to see a young woman kissing her date as he knelt before her. The other guests looked on with smiles. When they separated, the young man slid a ring onto her waiting finger before they kissed again. Cora beamed at the affectionate display. She turned to see Jamie looking on at the happy couple, his brows furrowed and lips pursed.

"Are you all right?"

Jamie's eyes found her, and his lips went up in a small smile. "Yeah... I am."

It was Cora's time to look at him skeptically. "You wanted to ask—" The vibrating against her leg caught her off guard. "Excuse me." She fished the cell out of her bag to silence it, but at the name on the caller id, her eyes widened, and her hand stilled. "It's Erin. I have to take this," she said, looking up at Jamie.

"It's fine," Jamie reassured her. He watched her move away from the table, and his face fell in disappointment.

"Hi, sweetie. How are you?"

"Mom," came her daughter's wobbly voice through the speaker. It sounded as if she had been crying. Cora's heart froze midbeat at the anguish in her daughter's voice.

"Erin, what's wrong?" she asked.

"Oh, nothing," her daughter replied, her voice coming out high-pitched. "I just... I miss my old life— you and Dad, Jules, and Brian..."

Cora's lips folded in on each other before she released them and sighed. "I know, sweetie. Sometimes I miss our old life too," she confessed, looking out into the darkness.

"Why isn't there a do-over button, Mom?" Erin hiccupped.

Alarm bells went off in Cora's head. "Sweetie, please tell me you're not drunk," she implored.

There was a short pause that felt like an eternity to Cora before her daughter responded.

"I'm not drunk. I've just had a few drinks...but I'm not drunk."

Erin's response did little to lessen the worry Cora felt.

"I can't believe Dad put our family through this. He betrayed us all, Mom."

"I know, sweetie, but we have to learn to move past it and try to get on with our lives," Cora appealed.

There was another pause before Erin replied, "I don't know if I can ever get past this... this hurt, Mom," Erin whimpered.

Cora felt her heart shatter at the vulnerability in her daughter's voice. "I know it's hard, sweetie, but you'll have to learn to forgive your father for what he did."

"No," Erin spoke firmly. "I will never forgive him for what he did. As far as I am concerned, he is dead to me."

"Erin," Cora cautioned. "He is still your father." When her daughter didn't immediately respond, Cora released a tired breath. She hugged her arm across her chest, trying to ward off the cold seeping into her bones and causing the small hairs at her nape to stand at attention.

"He didn't think about you or me when he chose to have an affair with our housekeeper, no less. Why should I think about him now?" Erin seethed.

Cora sighed. She didn't know what else she could tell her daughter to get her to forgive her father. It was, after all, Joel's choice to betray the family he already had the way he did, but that didn't mean she wanted her daughters going on hating the man that she knew loved them more than anything despite his shortcomings. She also didn't want them to be bitter and take that bitterness into their relationships.

"Sweetie, why don't you come to Oak Harbor for a while? I'm worried about you, and I think a change in setting might just be good for you," Cora implored.

"I-I...I can't right now."

"Why not?" Cora waited patiently for her daughter's response.

"I just can't right now, Mom," Erin replied.

"Okay... but I want you to know that you will always have somewhere to go to get away when life seems like it's too much. I'll always be here for you, sweetie."

"Thanks, Mom. I appreciate that and you," Erin said gratefully.

Cora beamed affectionately even though her daughter wasn't able to see her expression. "You're welcome, sweetie."

"There's something that I need to talk to you about... something I've been going through."

Cora perked up. "What is it? Is it something serious?"

"I can't say over the phone... I shouldn't have said anything. Forget I said anything," Erin backtracked.

"No. You should. Maybe I can help you," she reasoned.

"It's nothing, Mom. I gotta go. My friends are calling me."

"All right, sweetie. Please stay safe and don't drink anything else. I love you, and I'm here for you," she rushed out to say before her daughter could hang up on her.

"Love you too, Mom. Bye." With that, there was a click as Erin ended the call.

Cora released a heavy sigh before turning back to the restaurant. She didn't know she could miss the warmth this much as it thawed her from the inside out.

"I'm sorry about that," she apologized when she got to the table.

"That's fine," Jamie assured her lovely before asking, "Is everything okay?"

"I'm worried about Erin," she replied, her brows pulling down into a frown.

"Want to talk about it?"

Cora looked up at Jamie, his undivided attention on her.

Bittersweet Memories

"It's fine," she dismissed. "What was it that you wanted to ask me?" Her heart began to beat with anticipation once more.

"It's not important," he responded with a smile that barely reached his eyes.

"Oh..." Cora replied, unsure if she should feel disappointed or relieved that he hadn't asked. She finally picked up her fork and cut into her dessert, which had started melting, leaving a pink trail across the plate. She raised her fork to her mouth and pulled off the sweet confection. It was still good, but she couldn't concentrate on the treat as her mind ran away with thoughts about her family's dilemmas and the one she was currently sitting across from.

She had some important decisions to make.

"Ready to go?" Jamie asked after they'd finished their dessert.

"Yes," she replied.

After collecting their coats at the front, the two walked out into the chilly air toward Jamie's Ford. He helped her up into the passenger side before taking his seat beside her and pulling out of the parking lot.

The ride home was silent as the two got lost in thought. Cora felt guilty for the way the evening had gone. She'd been so caught up with worry that she had hardly enjoyed the special evening Jamie had planned for them, and she had inadvertently ruined his evening as well.

She looked over at his side profile and noticed the slight tick in his jaw before they ventured lower to his hands, tightly grasping the steering. She turned her head to look out the darkened window at the shadowy figures illuminated a fraction by the headlights of the vehicle. She gulped fearfully as she thought about her impending decision.

When they made it back to the house, Jamie helped her down from the vehicle and walked her up the few steps and across the porch to the front door. Cora abruptly turned to him.

"Can you sit with me for a bit?" she asked.

Jamie's eyes widened in surprise, but he quickly tapered them as he replied, "Sure."

Cora led him to the porch swing, and the two sat in silence. As the swing oscillated slowly, Cora opened her mouth, trying to find the words to say but each time she snapped her mouth shut, her heart beating with anxiety. She could feel his dark gaze on her, but she forced her head to remain straight as she stared across the porch railing. She finally garnered the strength to speak.

"Jamie, I don't want you to take this the wrong way. It isn't my intention to hurt you because I love you so much... I can't even express how much." She drew in a deep breath before releasing it slowly. Her hand wound tightly around the rope of the swing for support. "With everything that's been happening in my family... you're right. It has been taking a toll on me physically and mentally, and it has been affecting our relationship. I think it would be better if we put a pause on this, at least until I can figure out how to help my daughters and... deal with my mom on the verge of dying. I can't be there for you like I want to, and so I think it's better that we put the brakes on this for a bit."

Cora turned cautious eyes toward Jamie, who was now staring straight ahead. His Adam's apple bobbed as he swallowed.

"I can't say I agree with your decision because I'm not. But I will respect your decision," he spoke evenly. Slowly, he rose to his feet and turned to her.

Cora looked up at him as her heart grew heavy. A tear slid down her cheek. "I'm sorry," she spoke with anguish.

Jamie held out his hand for her to take. Cora placed her hand in his, the warmth igniting her. Jamie pulled her up and pulled her into an embrace. "It's okay," he soothed, running his palm over her hair as her cheek rested against his chest. "It's okay," he repeated.

The two separated after a few minutes, and Cora looked up at him, her eyes glistening. "I will always be there for you, Cora," he spoke reassuringly before bending his head and placing a kiss on the side of her mouth. "Happy Valentine's." He smiled.

"Happy Valentine's," Cora returned with a smile of her own.

She watched him as he descended the few steps. She watched him as he pulled a small box from his pocket, the little lantern lights along the path bright enough to illuminate the glistening piece of jewelry he pulled out before settling it back in the confines of the box. He shook his head as he snapped the box shut and put it back in his pocket. Jamie stepped up into his truck and slowly pulled away from the house.

More tears ran down her cheek as Cora watched him leave. It felt as if he had taken her heart with him, and for the umpteenth time, she wondered if she was making the right decision.

Chapter Nineteen

Jules was going out of her mind. She hadn't spoken to Noah for the past two days. He'd left the cookout disappointed after she'd told him in no uncertain terms that she would not be moving to South Carolina with him. It was driving her crazy, wondering where he was or what he was doing. She hadn't dared to ask her mother if he had checked out of the inn as she wasn't prepared to deal with the questions that would follow. However, Cora hadn't mentioned that he had, which left her with some hope that he was still in Oak Harbor — just not speaking to her. She still had another two days to go until her next OBGYN appointment, but to wait that long to know if he was still here or what his plans were did not feel like an option.

Her vibrating cell shook her out of her reverie. She hurriedly picked it up off the low table where her hand had been resting. The number was unfamiliar, but it had the same 786 area code as the one her father had called her from over two weeks ago. Jules's brows furrowed in annoyance. Her jaw clenched as she pressed the answer button.

"Hello?"

"Hi, sweetheart. How are you?"

"What do you want, Dad?" She ignored his question entirely.

There was a sharp intake of breath on the other end of the line before Joel responded. "I just...um... I was just calling to see how you were," he fumbled.

"I thought we established that you lost that privilege to know anything about my personal life since we last spoke," Jules replied, her eyes rolling heavenward. She knew she was acting petty— like a child, but she didn't care. There was no way she was allowing him back into her life so easily.

She heard her father sigh defeatedly. "I know words aren't enough to make up for what I did to you, to your mother, and your sister, but... I would like a chance to make it up to you, Jules," he pleaded.

The regret and desperation in his voice tore at Jules's heart and resolve. A single tear slipped down her cheek. "I don't know if you deserve another chance to be in my life, Dad," she admitted, her voice wobbling.

"Jules," Joel begged.

"I didn't deserve a father who chose to break up our family... you broke Mom's heart. Do you know that?" The tears cascaded down her cheeks this time as she unleashed her pain and anger on her father.

"I know. I'm trying to make up for it all— to make amends," he spoke solemnly.

Jules fought the urge to deliver a low blow to her father. She wanted him to hurt— to suffer as much as he had caused her to. Their family was left in shambles because of his actions. She didn't owe him squat.

"Look, Dad, it's going to take more than a few phone calls for me to even consider forgiving you, and quite frankly, I don't know if I want to. I don't owe you anything."

There was a long pregnant pause.

"That's fair. I should have thought about that before I called. But I promise I will make it up to you," he said earnestly.

"Bye, Dad."

"Bye, sweetheart—"

Jules held the phone in a death grip as she brought it from her ear. Her day had effectively gone from okay to worse. She looked out at the landscape. The vegetation was slowly making its comeback. Tufts of green grass covered the landscape with only a few brown spots.

Sighing, she slipped the comforter from around her shoulders and walked up to the banister to stare out at the bay. The water glistened as the afternoon sun burst through the barrier of the voluminous rolls of cottony clouds blanketing the sky. She could make out the mast and sails of a few boats on the horizon. Lush evergreens bordered the rest of the property, obscuring the view of the Cascade Mountains.

As serene as the scene before her was, it did little to calm the turmoil in her mind. Releasing a heavy breath, she descended the few steps and made her way along the concrete path leading toward the west end of the property. The tire swing attached to the Garry Oak caught her attention, and she diverted toward it. She ran her hand over the ridges in the tire before running them along the roughened rope, testing its integrity. She drew back the tire before releasing it, allowing it to swing back and forth. She wasn't sure why she'd done it, but it had a calming effect on her that she appreciated at that moment.

After a couple more swings, she returned to the path, pushing forward toward the inn. She came up to the back of the building. Jules stood in her spot admiring the three-story colonial-style house that had been successfully converted into an inn and attracted people from all over the country who wanted to experience the simplicities of a small town but still have the choice to enjoy outdoor activities and have a good night out on the town.

Jules walked toward the front of the building and up the steps to the wide-open porch. She pushed open the double French doors and walked into the large foyer. The wide sliding windows allowed for self-illumination. She especially liked the grand double staircase that led up to the first floor and the crystal chandelier hanging right above it, the waterfall tiers shimmering to create an air of elegance.

"Hi, Jules."

Her head turned with a snap of her neck to see Marg walking toward her with a smile on her lips.

"Hi, Marg," she greeted back. "Is my mom here?"

The woman stopped a few inches in front of her. "Yes. She's in the office. We were going over the books, but I need to find Olivia."

"Olivia, that's your assistant, right?"

"That's right," Marg replied with a nod. "I need to get some feedback about the guest list. You can go in. I'm sure she'll be glad to see you." She inclined her head to the side, her gaze fixing on the office door before turning back to Jules with an encouraging smile.

"Thanks," Jules replied, making her way toward the office while Marg took the nearest staircase up to the second floor.

Jules lightly rapped on the wooden door before turning the knob and pushing her head through. "Hi, Mom. Are you busy?"

Cora looked up from the ledger she was pouring over. "Hi, sweetie, I'm not too busy for you," she said as she removed her glasses and set them on the desk. "What's up?"

"Um... can we go for a walk?"

"Sure," her mother agreed, rising from the chair and walking around the desk to join her at the door.

The two walked toward the back porch and down the steps. They walked across the lawn toward the gazebo a few feet away. Jules slowly sank into the plush cushion of the wicker chair while her mother settled on the sectional on the opposite side.

"I wish we had one of these back at the house," Jules said after a prolonged period of silence.

"I do too," Cora said with a short chuckle. "So, what did you want to talk to me about?"

"Dad called again."

"Oh," Cora responded, sounding surprised. "What did he say?"

"He said that he wanted me to give him a chance to make it right," Jules replied, her face deepening into a frown.

"I take it from your expression you said no," Cora assessed.

Jules's eyes fluttered shut, and she pinched the bridge of her nose as she breathed in deeply before releasing it through her mouth. "I want to keep on hating him for what he did," was her answer that came out muffled as her palm covered her lips. Her confession hung in the air for a few more seconds before her hand fell from her face. "But my heart won't let me, and I miss him...so much." Her eyes slowly opened to look at her mother with a defeated expression. Cora stared back at her with understanding.

"He is trying to make amends, Jules. As much as what he did was despicable, I know he never meant to hurt you and Erin. He loves you, girls, more than anything," Cora said encouragingly. "Just give him a chance."

Jules looked away from her mother's beseeching eyes as she pondered her words. She did miss him, and it was that guilt of wanting him in her life even after what he had done that had filled her with anger, but maybe it was time to let go of all that and try to give him a chance. If not for herself, then for her unborn child. Instinctively her hand came up to rest protectively against her rounded tummy.

"I'll think about it," she conceded.

Her mother inclined her head in acceptance of her decision. "There is one thing that I need to talk to you about."

Jules stared at her mother questioningly.

"It's about Noah."

The mention of his name tied her stomach in knots. *Had he left?* "What about Noah," she asked, playing it cool.

Cora stared at her for a bit, her eyes filled with caution before she replied. "I know your father's betrayal scarred you, but I don't want you to let it affect your relationship with Noah."

"Oh," came her staccato response of relief.

Cora's brows furrowed in confusion at her reaction.

"It's funny you should mention not allowing my feelings to be swayed by what Dad did," Jules said with a curt laugh. "It so happens that I thought Noah had turned out to be just like Dad. That's why I didn't want to talk about him. Boy, was I wrong about him... on so many levels."

Cora continued to stare at her daughter, confusion written all over her face. "Why don't you start from the beginning?" she suggested.

Jules nodded. "I met Noah back in Seoul. He was on leave from the army. We got to know each other and decided to move our relationship forward. One thing led to another, and um..." Jules averted her eyes as she fumbled for words to explain how she came to be pregnant. "Then this happened," she finally finished. Cora's gaze rested on her hand, rubbing her tummy.

"By the time I found out I was pregnant, Noah had been deployed, and I had no way to get in touch with him. He did give me his parents' contact information, but then I called, and a girl answered, claiming to be his fiancée."

Cora sucked in a surprised breath.

"That's when I decided that we— the baby and I— didn't need him, and I called you," she continued, peeking under her lashes at her mother. Cora nodded slowly, prodding her to continue. "It turns out I was wrong because the girl is an ex who cheated on him, and he'd ended the relationship long before we met. I feel like a fool for not getting to the bottom of things instead of just assuming the worst," she admitted, shaking her head in regret.

"Well..."

Her eyes swung back to her mother.

"I'm glad you finally trusted me to tell me what happened." Cora looked appreciatively back at her daughter. "I like Noah. He seems to be a very respectable young man, and from my observations, it's evident he has feelings for you. However, the important question is, how do you feel about him?"

"I do have feelings for him, but... I'm scared," Jules responded, her blue eyes filled with vulnerability.

"You are still young, but so was I when I fell in love with your father. You deserve to be happy, sweetie, and if that is with Noah, then go for it. If it isn't, I'll be here for you all the way," Cora said encouragingly.

The corners of Jules's mouth lifted into a smile. "Thanks, Mom."

Her mother smiled back.

"Speaking of happiness, Jamie is deeply, I mean madly in love with you," Jules said, sporting a wide grin. She noticed the rosy tint to her mother's cheeks, and her lips widened further. "I know it didn't seem like it before, but I like Jamie. I think he's good for you."

"Oh, you do now, do you?" Cora questioned.

"I do," Jules repeated.

Her mother's smile waned. The sparkle that had brightened her blue-gray eyes dimmed. "I love Jamie too. However, I thought it was best we take a break. With everything that's

Bittersweet Memories

happening with Mom's illness, you about to have a baby, and Erin... I just didn't think I would have enough time to focus on our relationship, and I didn't want to burden him with ev—"

"Mom," Jules said, raising her hand to cut off Cora mid-sentence. "That is insane. You can't just choose to push away the one thing that makes you the happiest."

"No, honey. You, Erin, and my family make me the happiest," Cora retorted.

Jules gave her a deadpan look. "You know what I mean."

Cora sighed. "I don't want to burden him," she spoke softly.

"Mom, you have to give him a chance to be there for you. I don't know if you've noticed, but you have been way more open with Jamie than you had ever been with Dad. Don't shut him out now," she implored.

"I was happy with your father, too, for many years," Cora defended.

"I know, Mom. I was there too. Remember? But this... this feels more genuine, more open. I've noticed how freer your laughter is. I see how your eyes light up whenever he's around, and just I don't know... your body language is just different—lighter."

Cora's widened eyes stared at Jules as if it was the first time she was seeing her. "When did you get to be such a grown-up... and so wise," she marveled.

Jules grinned back at her mother as she proudly stated, "I think spending so much time with Grandma has had its benefits of making one wise."

Cora nodded. She rose out of her seat and walked over to her daughter. Jules gently pushed up from her seated position just in time to receive her mother's hug. "I am proud of you, sweetie. I want you to know that," she said against her temple. "I love you so much."

Jules smiled. "I love you too, Mom." For the first time in a long while, she truly believed that everything would be okay.

Chapter Twenty

"Jules, Noah's here!"

Jules's heart thundered. First, she rested the book she was reading, *What to Expect When You're Expecting*, on the armrest of the sofa she sat on. Then, slowly, she rose to her feet, holding on to the back of the chair for support. She drew in a deep breath and released it before walking off. Her breath came in rapid succession, and her chest rose and fell in pursuit of air. The hallway somehow felt longer than it was. Her brows drew together in question. She'd made the twenty-minute walk to the inn and back but hadn't been this winded. She wondered if it was something to worry about.

Her heart skipped a beat at the sight of Noah. His back was to her, and his head bowed, listening to Cora. Jules took the time to catch her breath and examine him. He wore a polo shirt stretched across the vast expanse of his shoulders and lying snugly across his broad back and down his lean waist. His brown hair had grown. It was now a wild mass of curls on top of his head.

Jules cleared her throat, gaining their attention. Noah's

Bittersweet Memories

head snapped up, and he turned in her direction. "Hi," he greeted, the sliver of a smile on his lips and his eyes staring at her with caution.

"Hi," she greeted back.

"I'm going to check on Mom— make sure everything's okay," Cora injected. She walked down the hall and made her to Becky's room.

Jules tore her gaze away from where Cora had disappeared to settle on Noah, watching her with apprehension.

"I thought you left," she shared.

"I didn't. I've been here the whole time. I'm sorry I didn't reach out sooner. I just needed time to think."

"What did you have to think about?" Jules pushed.

"About staying here... with you and the baby."

Jules's eyes widened, and her mouth popped open.

"I bought a few things that I thought would be good for the baby," he continued, not giving her a chance to recover from his initial statement. "Just wait here." Noah stepped through the door and headed for his car, leaving Jules wondering what he was up to. She drew closer to the door to see. Her eyes became saucers, and her hand slid to her throat as she watched him maneuver the steps while holding a box with a picture of a bassinet on the front.

Noah rested the box by the door before straightening up. "The sales rep suggested I buy the bassinet as the perfect choice for a newborn." He nervously scratched the back of his neck as he observed her face

"I got a crib too," he stepped in to say when still no words left her lips.

Jules's mouth dropped open again. She watched him head to the rented car and pull out a bigger box than before.

"Where should I set these up?" he asked after setting the box on the ground. He looked at Jules expectantly.

"Um... they can go in my room."

Noah nodded and proceeded to take one of the boxes to her room. Jules walked ahead, and when they got to her door, she held it open for him. Then, she waited by the door while he went for the other box.

Noah's gaze darted around the space in her bedroom. "We can set up the bassinet by your bed and put the crib in that corner." He pointed to the furthest corner away from her bed.

"Um, why don't we leave that for now? The baby's not due for another six weeks or so," she suggested.

Noah paused for a few seconds, his eyes contemplative. "Okay," he agreed.

"Have you eaten lunch?"

"Uh...no," he replied.

Jules smiled shyly. "Would you like to go to lunch...with me?"

His green eyes widened in surprise at her request. "Yes. I would."

Jules's heart jolted with a mixture of angst and excitement. "We can go by Willberry Eats. They should still be serving lunch now."

Noah pondered the suggestion, then nodded his agreement.

Jules reached for a sweater to cover her bare arms. She informed her mother where she was heading before setting off with Noah. They walked in comfortable silence. Jules took time admiring the picturesque path. No fresh, colorful blooms had erupted yet, but the low shrubs formed a winding green barrier on either side of the paved path they traversed. They walked past the inn ten minutes later and made their way to the restaurant, another two minutes away. It was an old barn remodeled to appear more modern and refined. The wooden exterior retained its rustic look, but large windows and a glass door gave it a modern touch.

Noah pushed open the door and allowed her to enter first.

The furnishing of the interior offered a relaxed, homely feeling. Stained wooden tables and chairs were evenly spaced throughout the room, lamps hung low from the high gable roof, and the ceiling fans ran the length of the room, attached to the rafter beams.

"Hi, Jules." Suzie, one of the waitresses, spotted her and waved. The bubbly young woman walked over to them.

"Hi, Suzie," Jules greeted. "Can we have a table?"

"Sure thing," Suzie replied eagerly.

Jules and Noah followed her to a table closer to the back.

"I'll let your aunt know you're here."

"Oh, that's fine. I don't need any fussing over," Jules assured the young woman.

"Okay," she replied. "What can I get you two?"

"I'll have the bouillabaisse," she ordered.

Suzie turned to Noah with a friendly smile. "And for you?" she asked.

"I think I'll have the same," he responded with a grin.

"All right. Coming right up." Suzie turned and walked toward the kitchen.

"So..." Jules looked at Noah to see his intense gaze on her. It felt as if he was looking into her soul. She felt her heart rate teeter over the edge, and she averted her gaze as she felt her cheeks warm over.

"Your hair looks lighter, more golden," he observed.

Her eyes widened in surprise that he had noticed that infinitesimal difference as her hair had only gone a shade lighter. "A product of this pregnancy," she revealed.

"I like it."

This time her blush permeated more than her cheeks.

"Here you go. One bouillabaisse for you and one for you," Suzie interrupted their conversation as she placed their dishes before them.

The spicy, fishy aroma filled Jules's nostrils and caused her mouth to spring water in anticipation of her first bite. The baby moved around in her tummy as if she was about to eat. She eagerly dipped the spoon into the stew before bringing it to her lips. She sighed in satisfaction at the fresh taste of the fish meat and the tangy, spicy flavor of the seasoned stock mixture.

"This is good," Noah complimented.

"Mhmm," she agreed.

The two kept their conversation light as they enjoyed the meal together.

"You need to try this," Jules encouraged, holding out her fork with a piece of the chocolate cake she'd ordered after.

"You know I'm not a fan of sweets," Noah reminded her.

"Oh, come on— just one bite. Please," Jules coaxed.

After a beat, his head descended, and he opened his mouth to envelope the piece of cake. Then, after a few slow bites, he responded with an impressed look. "You were right. It tastes great."

"Why don't you have some more?" She pushed another forkful of the confection before his face.

"Nuh-uh," he declined with a shake of his head. "One bite is enough for me."

"Please," Jules begged. Her lips turned down in a pout as she gave him sad puppy eyes.

Noah smirked. "You really know how to manipulate a guy, don't you?"

Jules's lips threatened to turn up into a smile, but she managed to hold on to her pitiful expression as she kept the fork before his mouth.

After a few challenging seconds, Noah sighed. "Fine, I'll have another bite if it wipes that look off your face," he gave in, taking the forkful of cake into his mouth once more.

Jules's lips broadened into a triumphant grin.

"You two make such a lovely couple," a woman and her companion smiled at them from the table over.

Jules felt her cheeks flush, and she ducked her head.

"Thank you," she heard Noah respond.

"Make sure you cherish your time together. It can never be regained once lost," the woman encouraged.

"We will," Noah answered.

Jules looked up from under her lashes to see Noah smiling brightly back at her, his emerald eyes sparkling as if he knew a secret she didn't. Her heart beat wildly.

"Penny, for your thoughts?" Noah asked as they strolled along the path they had taken back to the house.

Jules turned to look at him. "I was just thinking how nice this is," she confessed.

"It is," Noah agreed. "I miss moments like these," he spoke after another short stint of silence. "We had a lot of moments like these back in Seoul when we were getting to know each other. But, then, we were more open."

"That's because we didn't have an unborn child in the mix and miscommunication to contend with," Jules expressed.

"True," Noah nodded.

At his abrupt stop, Jules turned to look questioningly at him.

"When I was away, all I could think about was how much I wanted to get back to you— to pick up where we left off," he spoke with seriousness.

Her heart raced as she listened to his confession.

"Knowing that we had started something new and promising and that it had the potential to transform our lives was what kept me going all those months. The thought of you waiting for me helped me hold on to hope, Jules," he confessed.

Jules's heart felt as if it would burst from how full it felt, listening to Noah confess that he had wanted more for them. When his fingers intertwined with hers, the warmth that spread from their connected hands up her arm seemed to radiate heat all over her body, and she felt like she would combust, mainly when his green eyes focused entirely on her.

"I would like it very much if we could start being us again," he spoke with hope. Then, at her look of hesitation, he rushed on to say, "We can take it as slowly as you want. I'm okay with that."

Jules could only see sincerity and affection in his eyes, and although her heart was prodding her to say yes, her brain was telling her to play it cautiously. She looked away from his probing eyes to collect her thoughts.

"I can't deny that I still feel strongly about you, Noah, but... so much has happened in the last couple of months." She sighed and slowly disentangled their hands. She noticed the look of disappointment on his face, and she quickly averted her eyes.

"I need some time to think about this."

"All right. I understand, and I will respect your decision, whatever it is. Just, please don't shut me out," Noah begged.

Jules shook her head. "I won't."

Noah hung back at the front door as she opened it. She turned to him with a smile. "I had a great time today."

"I did too," Noah replied with a knowing grin.

Without warning, she stood on her tippy toes and kissed his cheek before heading inside.

Chapter Twenty-One

"Oh girls, they wanna have fun. Oh girls, just wanna have fun..."

Cora bobbed her head, and her fingers tapped the steering wheel, matching the tempo of the music that filled the van while she and her sisters belted out one of their favorite Cyndi Lauper songs.

"Some boys take a beautiful girl..."

She laughed at Andrea, who sat shotgun, belting out the third verse into an imaginary mic. Her head rocked back and forth vigorously. Her hair became a wild mass atop her head as she tried to impersonate her rock idol.

Cora looked through the rearview mirror to see Jo bobbing her head to the music less violently than their sister. Her hand rested on the armrest of Becky's wheelchair. Securely strapped into the machine, their mother looked happy, and her light brown eyes showed mirth. A smile lifted the corners of Cora's mouth as she returned her attention to the road. The decision to take Becky on this road trip was already paying off an hour into their journey from Oak Harbor to Seattle, and of course, they consulted the doctor, who had agreed she could go. However, they still had another half hour before arriving at their destination.

"I can't believe I lived less than twenty minutes away from this place for all those years, and I've never visited."

Cora adjusted the car stereo volume and briefly looked at her sister with pursed lips before focussing her attention on the road again. "It happens. We get so busy that we forget or refuse to enjoy what we have." Her eyes sought out her mother, and their eyes connected in the rearview mirror. She felt the pang of regret but refused to let it consume her. Today was a day to have fun and make happy memories with Becky. She would not allow the weight of what was to come or the regret of yesterday to ruin their day.

"Yeah, I know what you mean." Andrea sighed.

Cora noticed the tight knot between her brows and her clenched hand in her lap. Reaching across the console, she rested her palm over Andrea's hand and lightly squeezed. "Let's make the most of what we have now." Then, feeling her sister's eye on her, she turned and gave her a bright smile.

"Look at this. It says it has an art plaza and collections cafe where you can watch them do glass blowing while you eat."

"Drea, I'm driving." Cora chuckled, swatting away the cell phone her sister pushed in her face. "And yes, I know. I went through their website. So, we're doing it all."

"Awesome," Andrea cheered.

The van buzzed past the high-rise apartments and business complexes along John Street before slowing down and stopping at the traffic light.

"Look, the Space Needle." Andrea pointed through the windshield at the tall tower breaking the skyline in the distance.

"Magnificent, as always," Jo chimed in.

Bittersweet Memories

Cora glanced over her shoulder at her sister and nodded in agreement.

A car horn behind her alerted her that the light had changed. Slowly, she pulled off and continued toward their destination.

"I just love the three-hundred-and-sixty-degree view from the top, especially seeing the Cascade Mountains. Gosh, isn't it beautiful?" Andrea smiled in wonder. She turned to look at her sisters and continued. "Do you remember the Jetsons?"

"You mean that cartoon about that family that lives in space, had a robot for a maid, and flew in space cars?" Cora asked.

"Yes, that one," her sister confirmed.

"I do because you and Jo used to monopolize the television every Thursday evening when I wanted to watch my program." Cora playfully narrowed her eyes at her sister.

"Well, your show had a rerun, and Mom said we could watch it because two trumps one." Andrea stuck her tongue out at Cora before a wide grin broke across her face.

Cora couldn't help the giggle that left her lips. "You're still so childish," she said with a short shake of her head.

"Am not." Andrea pouted.

It was Jo's turn to laugh at her sisters' bickering.

"Back to what I was saying, I read that the Space Needle inspired the Jetsons' space homes," Andrea informed them.

"I didn't know that, but thinking about it now, I can see it," Cora replied, nodding her head thoughtfully.

"Back when Charles and Nicholas were alive, they, me, and Tracy did the eight hundred and thirty-two steps climb to the top for the cancer research benefit. It was one of the worst mistakes we'd ever made. I felt like I was losing my mind going up." Jo chuckled at the memory, and her sisters joined in. "Although the descent wasn't half as bad, we got to experience it together." Then, after a short pause, she said wistfully, "I wish we still had moments like those."

Cora glanced in the rearview mirror to see Jo's head bowed. She looked over at Andrea, who had a knowing look. They knew that no matter how many years passed and the amount of joy, their little sister would constantly relive the pain of losing her husband and son all at once. It pained Cora to see her like this.

"We're here," Cora announced a few minutes later as they pulled up to the Chihuly Garden and Glass Museum. Andrea opened her door and stepped out onto the pavement. Jo released the harness, tethering Becky's wheelchair to the van floor, while Cora released the sliding door's lock. With a soft whir, the door slid open. Cora released the ramp, and Jo carefully guided their mother down it.

"I'm gonna park and meet you guys back here," she informed them. Her sisters nodded in understanding.

After parking at the Seattle Center's 5th Avenue N, she returned to the museum. The five-minute walk back gave her enough time to think. Her thoughts found their way to Jamie, and her heart twisted. She missed him— very much. Unlike other times, they'd only spoken briefly, twice after Valentine's Day. She missed their late-night talks, planning their dates— the future. She missed going to bed with his voice lulling her to sleep and waking up to his deep timbre in the mornings.

Spotting her family by the entrance, Cora schooled her expression. "You guys ready to go in?"

A few minutes later, they walked around the gigantic building with numerous exhibitions made from glass. Cora marveled at how true to form and reflective of reality the structures were. It was unconventional, but it was magnificent.

"The artist had a lot of time on his hands...how did he come up with all of this?" Andrea pondered.

Cora wondered as she stared at the polychromatic flowers

projected from the glass roof. The colors bounced off the plain white walls like a multicolored disco light. Her eyes lowered, and she turned her neck to glance at her mother. Becky's eyes fixated on the roof, and a smile was on her lips. This made Cora's heart swell with gladness. As long as her mother appreciated it, she was comfortable.

Fifteen minutes later, they were moving toward the glasshouse— the glue that brought everything together on the property. Cora's lips parted, and her eyes widened. The glasshouse was true to its name, with glass panels fitted and running from top to bottom and granting access to the natural light that brightened the room and highlighted the red and yellow glass flowers.

"I've never seen anything quite like this— it is unique and just...wow!"

Cora chuckled at her sister's struggle for words.

"Let's get a photo together. Here comes one of the photographers," Jo suggested.

After expressing their need to be photographed, the three sisters settled in a semi-arch around their mother. They smiled widely as they stared into the lens of the camera.

"You can pick them up on your way out. Just give them this card at the front desk," the photographer informed them, handing Cora a rectangular card.

"Thank you," she said appreciatively. Then, she turned to her sisters. "Let's go see the garden," she suggested.

They made their way toward the open garden area, with Jo guiding Becky's wheelchair. Cora gaped at the beautiful structures along the path. They were intricate in their design and what one would expect futuristic plant species would resemble. However, the fact that they blended so well with the organic elements of the garden was magnificent to her. Her hand reached out to touch one of the glass structures but quickly retracted as she remembered it wasn't allowed.

"I could kick myself. All these years of visiting the Space Needle and not once did I come here."

Cora looked at Andrea shaking her head with regret.

"At least we're here now," Jo jumped in, and Cora inclined her head in agreement.

"What does this look like to you?" Andrea asked, pointing at the massive ball-like structure suspended in the middle of the garden.

"Like the sun," Jo answered.

Cora agreed. The fact that it was a whole mass of yellow with a few orange streaks and was in the center of the garden where everything else seemed to revolve around it made sense.

Frantic shouting caught her attention. She looked around to see a small boy, who couldn't be more than four, run up to Becky.

"Hi, I'm Justin. What's your name?" the little boy asked with a wide grin that revealed his missing front teeth. His smile slipped, and his eyes squinted with confusion as he stared at an unmoving Becky.

"Justin, what did I tell you about running off like that?" the woman who seemed to be his mother asked as she came to a stop. She reached out and took his small hand in hers. "I'm so sorry if he bothered you," she said with an apologetic tone.

"That's okay," Cora assured her.

"Mommy." The little boy tugged his mother's hand to get her attention.

"Yes, Justin, what is it?"

The little boy turned his gaze back to Becky before staring at his mother. "That lady is weird," he replied, attempting to whisper. But they'd all heard him. Cora's gaze cut to her mother to see that the glimmer in her eyes had disappeared, and her lips had become a flat line.

"Justin, that is a mean thing to say," his mother scolded. She turned to give them another smile of apology before walking away from them, pulling her son along.

The air felt heavy after the mother-son duo left. Cora released a heavy breath as she struggled to lift her spirit. Andrea was looking anywhere but at them, and Jo's gaze was on Cora, pleading with her to do something.

"Why don't we go get something to eat? I'm starving." Everyone agreed, and they made their way to the cafe. They enjoyed the glass-blowing demonstrations while they enjoyed their meal.

They didn't make it home until the sun had already disappeared over the mountains. Cora brought her mother to her room, and Andrea assisted in getting her changed and onto her bed.

"Today was fun," Cora spoke as she sat on the bed, brushing Becky's hair. Andrea had left to prepare her liquid meal. Cora looked down at her mother to see a small smile on her lips as if she agreed with her. Cora beamed. Her mind flashed to what the little boy had said and how much it had affected her, knowing that many people were probably thinking the same thing about her mother, even if they didn't voice it. She wished there was so much more that could be done for Becky.

When Andrea stepped back into the room, Cora left and headed for the kitchen to get a snack. The doorbell ringing caught her attention, and she beelined for the door.

"Hi, Noah. How are you?" she greeted the young man standing at the door.

"Hi, Cora. I was hoping we could talk," he replied, slightly rocking from side to side.

"Come in," she invited, stepping aside. "I was about to get myself a cup of tea and maybe a cookie... or two."

Noah chuckled.

"Good. I got you to loosen up a bit," she said.

The two made their way to the kitchen, Cora put on the kettle, and Noah sat around the island. Cora set a cup of the steaming liquid before him and a plate with three sugar cookies before sitting across from him.

"So, what did you want to talk about?" she asked, taking a sip of her tea.

"Jules is ready to give birth soon. I was thinking about doing something nice for her," Noah replied.

"I've been thinking about that too," Cora said.

"Great, what do you have in mind?" Noah asked.

Cora smiled. "A baby shower."

Chapter Twenty-Two

"You look beautiful."
Jules stared at her mother through the mirror and made a face. "I don't feel beautiful," she replied lowly.

Cora walked up and placed her hands on her shoulders. Their eyes connected once more. "You are beautiful... more than you know," she affirmed.

Jules reached up and squeezed the hand on her shoulder as she smiled appreciatively back at her mother.

"Thanks, Mom."

Cora placed a kiss on her cheek. "I'm gonna go check on Mom."

Jules nodded and watched her mother exit her room. "All right, Jules, it's just one date. Nothing to be nervous about. We're just getting something to eat and... talk." She inhaled and exhaled slowly as she tried to calm her frazzled nerves. The last date she'd been on was with Noah— that was over eight months ago. She didn't know what to expect. She picked up the phone to cancel on him more than twice. *What if this was a mistake?*

What if she was only setting herself up for more heartbreak? She remembered how she'd shattered when she'd learned that Noah had a fiancée. She wasn't sure she was strong enough to go through another of those.

The slight kick against her tummy caught her attention, and a smile instantly curled her lips upward and settled her mood.

"Hi, sweetie," she cooed, rubbing her large tummy over the peach crochet dress she wore. "Your papa and I are going on a date." She grinned. The baby kicked against her palm. "You're excited about that, huh?" she asked, lifting her head to stare back at her reflection. "That makes one of us," she finished, her lips pressed inward.

She took the time to look over her appearance. The dress was snug across her bust and middle, bringing attention to her rounded belly before it flared off and stopped just below her knees. She'd taken her mother's advice and let down her blond hair to fall over her back and around her shoulders. She had gained weight on her arms, her cheeks looked a little plump, and her sandals were either tight or looked weird on her feet. It was enough to make her a little self-conscious.

The knock at her bedroom door pulled her away from her inspection. She turned to the door just as her mother's head peeped through. "Noah's here," Cora informed her.

"All right. Just give me two minutes, and I'll be out," Jules requested.

"Okay, sweetie," her mother accepted, but before she left, she repeated, "You are beautiful."

Jules gave her a grateful look. She walked over to the bed and took up her purse and jacket. She stopped at the mirror and did a once over. Then, inhaling deeply before releasing it, she turned and exited her bedroom.

The moment Noah saw her, his green eyes flashed wide,

Bittersweet Memories

and she noted his Adam's apple bob up and down as he gulped.

"Wow, you look amazing," he complimented, walking toward her. His eyes shone with admiration, and Jules felt warmth in her chest before it traveled to her cheeks.

"Thank you," she replied shyly. "You look amazing too," she returned, taking in the black button-up shirt Noah wore tucked into gray slacks that showed off his long, lean physique. His brown hair was curlier and complemented the boyish grin on his lips.

"Thanks. These are for you." Then, he presented her with a bouquet of white and yellow roses.

Jules reached for the roses and brought them up to her nose. "Thank you, they're lovely," she said demurely.

"The florist said yellow represents friendship, and white is for innocence and new beginnings," he informed her.

"I like that," Jules replied.

"I'll put these in water for you," Cora offered, moving from the stairs where she had been posted.

"Thanks, Mom." Jules passed the bouquet to Cora and turned to Noah.

"Shall we go?" he asked.

"Yes," she responded.

"Have a good time, you two." Cora smiled at them from the door as they made their way across the porch.

After opening the car door for Jules and allowing her to settle in, Noah got in the driver's seat and pulled out of the driveway. Jules let the cool, crisp air from the open window blow across her face and ruffle her hair as the car cruised through the town.

"Where are we going?" she turned to ask him when she noticed that they were getting closer to the waterfront.

Noah turned to her with a smirk. "You'll know soon enough."

Jules pushed her lips out in a pout as she stared at him from under her lashes.

A deep-throated chuckle erupted from his lips, the sound filling the caverns of the car like a newly found tune. She had to admit that she liked the sound of his laughter.

"That won't work on me. Although you do look cute doing it." Noah's lips lifted, and his bright eyes crinkled at the corners.

It was Jules's turn to laugh. "I remember you being a lot more…"

"What? More pliant?" Noah asked with a raised brow.

"That wasn't the word I was looking for, but… yes, I guess so," Jules responded with a smile.

"Don't worry. You've still got it," Noah assured her. "We're here."

Jules's eyes narrowed, but just as quickly, they widened in surprise, and she turned her head to stare at the building Noah was parking before.

"You took me to *le fleur-de-lis*?" she asked, barely able to contain her excitement.

"I'm guessing I did well?" Noah asked, an ear-splitting grin on his face.

Instead of answering his question, she asked, "How did you get a reservation here? This is a three-star Michelin restaurant with a wait list all the way back to fall."

"Let's get inside first, and I'll answer all your questions." Noah stepped out of the car and rounded the passenger side. He opened the door and held out his hand to her. Jules placed her hand in his. The warmth from where their hands touched then traveled up her arm and threatened to color her cheeks. She felt slight flutters in her stomach and wondered if they were butterflies or the baby moving around.

The two walked side by side toward the restaurant, but Noah stopped her before they entered.

Bittersweet Memories

Jules turned to look at him, her eyes questioning.

"I know I said it before, but I must repeat it. You look stunning." Noah's warm smile and sweet words filled her heart with hope.

Noah pulled open the door, and soft piano music streamed through it. As she stepped through the door, Jules gasped at the beauty before her. The restaurant was draped in deep red and gold hues, and the chandelier that hung from the ceiling in the center of the room shimmered as the crystals reflected the light, resembling a crown jewel. She walked further into the room, and her feet sank into the plush burgundy carpet beneath them.

"Welcome to *le fleur-de-lis*. How may I assist you?" a gentleman in a flawless black suit asked from a reservation table to the left.

"Hi. Reservations for two under McKinley," Noah spoke up.

The gentleman held up a tablet and tapped away at the screen before looking at them with a bright smile. "Please follow me. Your table awaits," he advised.

Jules self-consciously tugged her dress as she looked at the other women dressed in silk and chiffon. Their clothing alone screamed sophistication. She felt out of place. Noah's hand joined with hers, and their fingers intertwining caused her to look up. He was already staring back at her. "You're beautiful," he said with conviction.

"Here we are," the maître d' informed them, stopping at a table with only two chairs around it. "Your waiter will be with you shortly," he told them when they were seated and then left them alone.

"How are you feeling?" Noah asked a few seconds after the man left.

"Honestly?" Jules asked before pursing her lips. Noah inclined his head. "I feel... a little intimidated," she answered, raising her hand and showing a small space between her thumb and index finger.

"You don't have to be. You are single-handedly the most beautiful woman here," he said, his green eyes staring intently back at her.

The butterflies returned, and Jules ducked her head as she felt her cheeks warm.

"Hi, my name is Alistair. I'll be your waiter this evening. Can I get you something to drink while you go over our menu?" a young man as pristinely dressed as the maître d' asked.

"We'll have your best nonalcoholic cocktail," Noah informed him.

The young man bowed his head and left to get their drink order.

"You didn't tell me how you managed to score a reservation," Jules reminded him as they sipped on the sweet but tangy drink the waiter had just brought.

"You are relentless." Noah chuckled. "I know the owner of the parent restaurant back in Seattle. Well, actually, my parents do."

Jules nodded in understanding. "What do your parents do?"

"My mother is a housewife, but my dad runs the family hardware store, plus our farm."

"Sounds like a very busy man," she pondered.

"Yeah. Dad works very hard, but my older brother Jed, he's there too. He is Dad's second in command," Noah revealed.

Just then, their meals arrived, and Jules grinned gratefully at their waiter before taking a bite of her beef tenderloin. "Mhmm, this is so good." She sighed, eyes closed, as the butter-like texture of the beef infused by the spices used like rosemary and the slight tang of lemon grazed her tongue. Her eyes fluttered open, and she was taken aback to find Noah's green orbs fixated on her face. She blushed.

"So, does your brother also live on the farm?" Jules asked after a few more bites of her meal.

"He does with his family and my two younger sisters," Noah answered.

"And you're all close?" she asked, noting the smile on his lips.

"Yeah, we are," he answered. "They're annoying mostly." He pulled a face.

Jules was happy, but then her mind switched to her sister. Her happiness dimmed a bit. She and Erin used to be so close. Now, she didn't know where her sister was. She no longer called to tell her what was happening in her life. A dejected sigh slipped past her lips.

"Uh-oh. I don't like the sound of that," Noah said, staring at her with concern.

Jules looked away, watching the other guest have their meals while some chatted away. "I miss my sister," she confessed.

After more than a minute of silence, Noah responded. "Why don't you just call her?" he asked.

"She's not answering my calls. She hasn't been answering anyone, for that matter."

"I'm sorry to hear that, Jules," Noah said apologetically, reaching across the table to rest his hand atop hers.

"It's fine. I have enough to deal with as is," she assured him.

After taking care of the check, the two left the restaurant and walked along the pier. Jules inhaled the salty ocean air and brought her sweater closer to her chest.

"Here, take this." Noah shrugged off his jacket and placed it over her shoulder. Jules inhaled his scent, a mixture of soap, allspice, and his natural male musk. She pulled the coat closer to inhale more.

"If I don't get to tell you later, I had a great time," Jules said as they looked out at the darkened water and boats posted in the bay rocking lightly against the current.

"I had a great time too," Noah replied, turning to her with a wide grin, the glow from the overhead lamp illuminating his face. His face scrunched up. "Excuse me for a bit; my phone is set to ring only for emergency calls," Noah informed her as his hand dived into the pocket of his slacks.

"It's fine," Jules told him. Noah looked back gratefully. "It's my mom," he told her after checking the caller id. Jules bowed her head to her chest as she indicated it was okay.

"Hi, Mom," Noah greeted.

Jules watched him converse with his mother before his eyes turned to her. Naturally, this put her on high alert.

"My mom wants to talk to you," he said.

Jules widened her eyes, and her heart slammed against her chest as she took the phone.

Chapter Twenty-Three

"Hi," Noah greeted Jules as she sat under the gazebo by the inn waiting for him.

"Hi," she greeted back, smiling.

Noah took a seat beside her on the sectional. "Ready to do this?" he asked, placing the laptop on the low table before them.

Jules slowly nodded, her lips pursed and apprehension in her eyes.

"Relax. My parents will love you," Noah said with a reassuring grin.

"Are you sure? I mean, I did refuse to talk to your mother last night," Jules asked. She had declined the offer to talk to his mother, and she was sure the woman must have considered her rude. Noah had made up an excuse on the spot, but she was sure the woman hadn't bought it.

"They will," Noah repeated, his green eyes filled with conviction.

"Okay, I'm ready," Jules said, blowing her breath.

Noah pulled up the Skype app and pressed the call button.

After the third ring, the screen opened to a man and a woman filling it up, their faces eager and smiling.

"Hi, Mom, Dad," Noah addressed his parents.

"Hi, sweetie."

"Hi, Son," his father replied.

"This is Jules," he introduced, turning the laptop so Jules was more in the frame. "Jules, these are my parents, Evelyn and Ken."

"Hi." Jules waved shyly at them.

"Hi, Jules. I am so happy to finally put a face to the name." Evelyn smiled warmly at her.

"It is a pleasure to meet you, Jules," Ken added.

"It is a pleasure to meet you both," Jules returned with a smile of her own, feeling more at ease.

"Ooh, Noah, she is just adorable," Evelyn spoke excitedly, inciting a laugh from Noah and Jules.

"She is," Noah agreed, looking over at her with gleaming eyes.

Jules blushed. Ken excused himself after reiterating his pleasure in meeting her.

"So, Jules, Noah tells us that your due date is next month," Evelyn said, looking at her expectantly.

"Yes, that's right," she confirmed, her hand resting on her tummy.

"I can't wait to meet her. It's such a blessing to get a granddaughter finally. Noah's brother Jed has four boys," Evelyn informed Jules. "I can't wait to dote on her," the woman said, grinning expectantly. "Have you decided on a name?"

"No. Not yet," Jules told the older woman.

"Maybe I can help with a few suggestions," Evelyn offered.

"Um, I have a few that I'm thinking of choosing from already," Jules said.

"Oh. Okay," Evelyn replied, her chirpiness from earlier down a few decibels.

176

"You can still make the suggestions," Jules offered, feeling that she had hurt the woman's feelings.

"Oh no, that's fine. I'm sure you've already got the perfect name on your list." An awkward silence ensued before Evelyn spoke again. "You know, we never thought that a day like this would come."

Jules's brows twitched toward each other. "What do you mean?" she couldn't help but ask.

"Noah's break up with Dina— we never saw it coming," Evelyn answered.

Jules felt her heart clunk to the bottom of her chest.

"We had always believed that they would have gotten married. We even picked August's date last year, but they broke up, and to this day, neither of them has explained what happened. I was holding out hope—"

"Mom," Noah butted in, his voice bordering on a warning.

Evelyn laughed lightly, but the sound only made Jules more uncomfortable. "Oh well, I suppose that is all water under the bridge. You seem like a lovely young woman, so I'm happy to welcome you to the family." The woman beamed.

Jules returned the smile, although hers was more strained. It was evident that Evelyn was disappointed that Noah had broken up with Dina and that she probably would never accept her as much as she did the other woman. Disappointment settled in her chest.

"So, how long after the baby is born will you move to South Carolina?"

"Excuse me?" Jules asked, looking from the screen to Noah, who looked away guiltily.

"Oh. It seems I jumped the gun on that," the woman said apologetically. "But Noah's life is in South Carolina. He has his own house. Did he tell you?" The woman didn't give Jules time to answer, not that she was able to form words as she stared stupefied at the screen. "It'll be so nice to see the house filled with grandchildren and being able to have them near."

"Evelyn, I'm sorry, but I'm not moving to South Carolina," Jules interrupted.

The woman's brows jogged up her forehead, pulling her eyes wide apart.

"I'm not sure what you and Noah discussed, but I never agreed to move, and to be honest, I do not see myself leaving Oak Harbor anytime soon."

Silence ensued after her revelation.

"Mom, um, there's something that I gotta take care of. Maybe we can pick this conversation up later," Noah suggested, scratching the back of his neck.

"Okay, sweetie. Jules, truly, it was a pleasure meeting you," the woman said.

"It was a pleasure meeting you too, Evelyn," Jules returned. The moment the call went offline, Jules turned to Noah as she eyed him narrowly. "Why do your parents think I'm moving to South Carolina?" she seethed. "I thought we had this discussion. I'm not moving to South Carolina."

"I know. You made that perfectly clear," Noah threw back with frustration. He breathed in deeply before releasing it, deflating his shoulders. "I'm sorry. I should have said something to them before letting it get this far."

Jules eyed him for a few long seconds before asking, "Why won't you tell your parents why you broke up with Dina?"

Noah averted his eyes. "It's complicated."

"Enlighten me," Jules said, deathly calm.

"We were friends before we were a couple, and our parents are like family. So, I didn't want them to start looking at her differently," he expressed.

Jules's lips curled out dejectedly. That wasn't the answer she was expecting. She wondered again if she had made the right choice to give Noah a chance.

Bittersweet Memories

* * *

"Hi, Marg. What do you want me to do?" Cora asked as she stepped through the inn's double doors entering the foyer. She stared expectantly at her friend behind the receptionist's desk.

Marg looked up from the guest book she had been reviewing, and a smile graced her lips. Cora had suggested that they save the reservations for their guests using Google Organizer, but Marg had convinced her that it was more authentic and personal to record their guests' check-ins in that fashion.

"Hi, Cora. I'm glad you're here. Andrea's upstairs changing the linens on the beds and curtains," Marg informed her.

"What do you need me to do?" she asked.

"I need you to vacuum the carpets and couches," Marg instructed. "We have three guests arriving before the end of the week, and for all we know, one of them might be the travel critic."

"Are you sure a travel critic is here in Oak Harbor?" Cora asked, suspicious of the source of information.

"I am sure," Marg replied. "He visited the inn back on 8th Ave, and two days later, there was a review on the travel page, and they received three stars. We have to aim higher by being on target with everything. So, by the time he gets here, he'll have nothing to write other than to heap praises on the inn."

"All right then, let's get to work," Cora replied, heading for the storeroom for the vacuum cleaner. She made her way up the stairs just as Andrea came down them.

"I'm going to town to pick up a few art pieces," Andrea informed her.

"All right," she agreed.

Cora turned and made her way up the stairs. The first room she entered was one of the junior suites. Plugging the vacuum into the socket, she slowly moved the whirring machine across the carpet, allowing it to displace the dust and lint as it got sucked into the cavity.

When she finished vacuuming the couch, she believed the room could be a four-star hotel. She opened the double windows to let in the bright sunshine, illuminating the room. She stepped through the double French doors onto the balcony overlooking the garden. She spent a few minutes admiring everything before heading inside.

Within the next hour or so, Cora had finished. "Marg, I'm going for a walk," she told her friend.

"Okay."

Cora left through the back door and made her way toward the gazebo. As she neared the structure, her heart hammered against her chest at who was standing there— Jamie. Jamie, who'd had his back to her, turned to her as she approached. His eyes widened, and his lips parted.

"Hi," she greeted with a slight wave as she came to stand before him.

"Hi," Jamie greeted back.

"What are you doing here?" she asked him, looking around. "I mean..."

"I know what you mean," Jamie responded lightly. "I came to take some measurements of this gazebo for the second one we're making," he informed her.

"Oh, I forgot about that," Cora replied. "The guests really love this gazebo; it has been a great hit." She gestured with her hands toward the structure.

"Yeah, they do." Jamie laughed.

Cora missed that deep rumbling sound of his amusement and joy. Their eyes connected, and it was as if an imaginary line was holding them together.

"How have you been?" Jamie finally asked.

"Honestly?" Cora released a heavy breath. "I've been miserable," she confessed.

Jamie's head bowed forward before moving back up in understanding.

"I miss your calls. I didn't know how much I looked forward to them until I no longer had them." She folded her hands over her chest and hugged herself. "I miss your sweet texts," she softly whispered, looking down at her feet.

The light touch against her cheek caused her to lift her head just as Jamie's hand dropped to his side.

"I miss those too," he admitted. "I knew you needed your space, so I wanted to honor that."

Cora nodded her understanding. "I made a mistake," she admitted after a short pause, regret shining in her gray-blue eyes as she stared at him.

A sliver of a smile appeared on his lips. "Let's go for a walk," he suggested.

Cora took the hand he offered, feeling the warmth from their connection ignite a fire in her stomach. The two walked hand in hand toward the docks. As they came to a stop at the water's edge, they stopped and stared out at the blue-green water, calm and unassuming. Her gaze switched to the *Silver Bullet* safely docked and moving back and forth following the direction of the tide.

"I think I started falling in love with you when I saw how hard you worked on my father's boat, restoring it to its former beauty," she confessed, glancing at him. Cora turned fully to him. "It's been hard these last couple of months, but I want you to know that the thought of your love and support is what gets me through the days." A tear slid down her cheek.

"Hey, hey, don't cry," Jamie implored her. He tenderly cupped her face and used his thumbs to wipe the tears away.

Cora sniffled and continued as he held her to his chest. "It's what keeps me fighting for my family each and every day. It's the only thing that I've been able to depend on." She felt Jamie's lips graze her temple.

"All I want is for you to be happy, Cora," Jamie revealed. "I will always be there for you, Cora. I want to be your tower of strength, always." He pulled her face back and gazed into her eyes.

Cora slowly tipped upward and placed a kiss on his lips. "I don't know what I did to deserve someone like you, but I'm grateful," she spoke affectionately.

"I am thankful to have you in my life," Jamie returned, and Cora placed her head back on his chest.

After a few minutes of them staying that way, Cora spoke.

"I'm scared to lose Mom," she said solemnly. "I'm scared of so many things," she revealed.

"We'll figure it out together," Jamie said against her hair.

"I love you," Cora said lovingly against his chest.

"I love you too."

Chapter Twenty-Four

"What's wrong, sweetie?"

Jules's gaze swept up from the page in her book she had been staring at for the past five minutes to find Cora staring back at her with worry.

"I'm fine, Mom." She smiled.

Cora watched her carefully. "Are you sure?" she asked after some time.

Jules stared at her with a mixture of confusion and annoyance. "I am. Why do you ask?"

Cora didn't respond immediately. Releasing a breath, she sat up in the wicker chair. "I called your name twice, and you didn't respond. You've been staring at the same page for a while without blinking, and it made me wonder if something was bothering you."

"I was just thinking about Noah. It's not a big deal, though," Jules downplayed, staring past the porch rails and the fir trees to the glistening water, its deep blue color a reflection of the sky above.

"You miss him," Cora surmised. Jules's lack of response was

confirmation enough. "What's it been four days since he returned to South Carolina?" It was already the first week of March.

"Five," Jules corrected. She winced, and her mother grinned knowingly.

"You know it's okay to say you miss him, Jules. I've seen how you two have been acting around each other, and I can see that you're trying to work it out."

Jules inhaled a long, deep breath, drowning her lungs with air before releasing it. "I do miss him, but I'm also scared to," she confessed. Glancing over at her mother, she noted Cora looking at her expectantly. Jules turned her head back toward looking out at the water. "After our date the other day, I spoke to his parents, and they seem to think I'm moving to South Carolina after the baby is born."

"What? Are you planning to move?" Cora asked, alarmed.

"No." Jules shook her head vehemently. "Noah has a house... well, his grandfather willed him his house and six hundred acres of land." Her head swung around at her mother's sharp intake of breath. "That was my exact reaction. His parents want him to come home to take over running his grandfather's wheat farm."

"What did Noah say?" Cora asked.

"He said he wants to be wherever his baby is." Jules sighed dejectedly. "I'm afraid that if he ends up staying, he will resent me for it...resent our child." She turned sad eyes to her mother. "I don't want him to feel like I trapped him, Mom." A tear slithered down her cheek as her eyes shone with many more unshed ones.

"Oh, sweetie, I'm sorry you feel that way." Cora rose, walked over to her daughter, and pulled her into her arms. It was all Jules needed to let the dam burst.

"I don't know what I'm doing, Mom. It feels like I'm

making him choose between his family and this baby," Jules sobbed.

Cora pulled back and put her palms on either side of her daughter's face. She stared thoughtfully into her glistening blue eyes. "Listen to me, Julia. It is your choice to stay in Oak Harbor, and you should not feel guilty over that. If Noah chooses to stay here, too, that's his choice. He chose to stay. Do not beat yourself up over it. That young man adores you. He has a right to make his own choice. Don't. Push. Him. Away."

Jules stared at her mother with newfound admiration, and a small smile cracked her lips. "I love you, Mom."

Cora blinked in surprise. "I love you too, sweetie," she expressed. Then, pulling Jules's face closer, she kissed her forehead. "Everything will work out," she affirmed.

Coming from her mother's lips, Jules started to believe everything would work out.

"I'm going to check in on Mom for a bit."

"Okay," Jules replied, then watched her mother pull the back screen door open and enter the house. She lowered herself back into the rocking chair she had been sitting in and continued staring at the water. She felt the baby barely stir. Finally, her hand came up to rest on her tummy. "I miss him, too, sweetie," she said in a whisper.

The baby had been kicking a lot more since she entered her third trimester, but within the past couple of days, she only felt her movements a few times. At over eight months pregnant, Jules felt something was wrong. Still, her doctor had explained that it was perfectly normal for the fetus, especially if one or more stimuli went absent, which could affect its activities in the womb. Jules had then narrowed it down to her little girl missing her father.

Her vibrating phone caught her attention. She picked it up from the small table at her side and swiped up. Her heart leaped. A bright smile split her face when she saw the caller id.

"Hi," she breathed out.

"Hi," came Noah's instant reply. "How are my two favorite girls in the world?"

Heat crept up the back of her neck and into her cheeks. Butterflies collided against each other in her stomach. "I'm fine. Your daughter, however…"

"What's wrong?" Noah shot back worriedly.

Jules's lips lifted at the corners. "Well, she hasn't been her rambunctious self for a while now. I think she misses her dad."

Laughter erupted from the other end of the line, the deep throaty sound filling Jules with warmth. "You got me good," he said a few seconds after calming down.

"I aim to keep you on your toes," Jules snickered.

"That you do," Noah said.

Jules felt the baby's soft kick against her belly. She reached over and rubbed the spot. "She's kicking now. I think she knows it's you," she revealed.

"Switch to video call," Noah requested.

Noah's face popped onto her screen a few seconds later. His meadow-green eyes were already staring at her.

"Hi," he said smilingly.

"Hi," she managed to say. Another kick pulled her out of her stupor. "Suddenly, this one doesn't want to give me a break from her little feet." She almost grunted with a chuckle as she sat straighter in the rocking chair.

"Let me talk to her," he offered.

Jules brought the phone close to her belly.

"Hello, sweetheart, it's your daddy. I just want you to know I miss you, too, my little sprite. I'll be home soon to finish reading to you about Goldilocks, I promise," he cooed.

It felt as if a stampede had gone off inside her as the baby flitted from side to side, her little feet beating rapidly against Jules's flesh. She brought her hand under the curve of her belly and rubbed.

Jules brought the phone up to her face. "She's going to hold you to that promise."

Noah nodded in agreement. "And what about her mother?" he asked, his gaze direct.

"What do you mean?" Jules asked with a raised brow.

"I mean, is it only Petunia that misses me?"

"We are not calling her that." Jules chuckled with a quick shake of her head.

Noah smiled. "Not even as a middle or pet name?" His green eyes shone with mischief.

"Not a fat chance," Jules declared.

Noah stared at her with intrigue. Jules squirmed at the intensity in his eyes. "You still haven't answered my question," he reminded her.

Jules swallowed hard and averted her eyes. She nibbled her bottom lip. Then, finally, she turned to face him. Her eyes shone with vulnerability. "I do miss you... a lot," she confessed. "I don't know if it's pregnancy hormones, but I wish you were here now," she finished lowly.

Noah said understandingly. "I miss you, too, Jules... a lot," he admitted.

Jules smiled bashfully.

"I'll be back in two days; after that, I'm not leaving again until our little Petunia is born."

"We are not naming her Petunia." Jules pouted before breaking into laughter. Noah joined in.

* * *

"Why don't we do something fun?"

Jules lowered the book she had been trying to read since yesterday to stare at her mother. "Like what?" she asked.

Cora tapped her chin thoughtfully. Suddenly her face

brightened. "We should have a mother-daughter spa day," she suggested, her voice filled with excitement.

"I don't know," Jules hesitated.

"It'll be fun," Cora promised, staring expectantly at her daughter.

"Okay," Jules caved. She thought it would be nice to get out of the house for a while. In addition, she had not been feeling her best. Her protruding tummy, swollen ankles, and fuller cheeks made her feel rather unattractive. Maybe a day at the spa could help with that.

"Excellent," Cora said triumphantly. "Andrea is by the fire station, and Jo is at Willberry Eats, but I'm sure the nurse will be able to manage with Mom for a few hours until we get back."

Jules nodded.

Forty-five minutes later, Jules was sitting in a cushioned chair, her feet soaking in warm water as bubbles jetted up, forming a thick layer of white around her ankles. A woman sat on a low stool, painting her fingernails a soft pink color.

"Aren't you glad we chose to do this?"

Jules rotated her neck and smiled in agreement at her mother in the chair opposite hers.

"How do you feel?" Cora asked.

Jules thought about it before offering an answer. "Less stressed," she finally responded.

"Good," Cora replied with a nod. "After we're done here, let's visit the hair salon and get a wash and a blowout."

"Okay," Jules agreed, getting into the pampering. She leaned back in the chair and closed her eyes for a short nap.

When they finished at the spa, the two women made their way down the paved walkway of downtown Oak Harbor. They stopped at a few storefronts to admire their window displays before walking into the salon.

"Welcome to Beautiful Hair," a woman sitting in front of a computer at a corner desk greeted them with a warm smile.

Bittersweet Memories

"Hi, we have an appointment for Cora Hamilton and Julia Avlon," Cora said to the woman.

The woman typed something on the computer. "Your stylist will be with you shortly. Meanwhile, you can take a seat," the woman informed them.

Jules's brows narrowed suspiciously as she followed her mother toward a black sofa resting against the wall. The two settled on it before Jules turned to look at her pointedly.

"You made an appointment? When?" she asked in a hushed tone.

"I called them when you went to the bathroom back at the spa, and they said they had two openings," Cora answered with a strain in her voice.

Jules eyed her mother under her lashes but finally released a breath and accepted the explanation. Then, she turned her attention to the other women sitting in their chairs while the stylists did wonders to their hair.

Half an hour later, they were both in a chair getting their hair washed. Jules decided to cut a few inches off that brushed the middle of her back. When the stylist finished, her hair hung just below her shoulder.

"You look stunning, sweetheart," her mother complimented.

Jules smiled in acceptance. "You look stunning," she returned the compliment, taking in her mother's lustrous blond main with strawberry highlights. "I like the highlights."

"Thanks," Cora replied. "We still have a bit more time before the nurse has to leave." Cora looked at the watch on her wrist. "Why don't we make this a full mother-daughter day out and go try on some dresses?" she suggested.

"Okay," Jules agreed. "But not before we get something to eat. I'm starving."

"Let's get some food in you." Cora chuckled.

Another hour passed before Cora and Jules were driving

away from downtown and making their way onto E Pioneer Way, and after another fifteen minutes, they were pulling past the inn on their way to the main house.

"I had fun today, Mom. Thank you." Cora turned to Jules, who smiled back at her appreciatively.

"You're welcome," Cora said.

Pulling into the driveway, Jules jumped out of the car and reached for the bags in the back.

"You go on to the house. I'll take those in."

"All right," Jules replied.

"Jules."

She turned back to her mother.

"You look beautiful," Cora murmured lovingly.

Jules looked down at the soft pink chiffon off-the-shoulder dress her mother had convinced her to wear home after their purchase. Although she had to admit, the dress was beautiful and accentuated all her assets well.

She grinned and turned to head inside. She pushed open the door and noted how quiet the house was. She guessed that her aunts were home. She opened her grandmother's door, and her brows drew together.

"What's wrong?" Cora asked behind her.

"Grandma's not in her room."

"Why don't you check the living room?" Cora suggested.

Jules walked further down the hall. As she drew closer to the living room, she realized no sound was coming from the TV. Still, she stepped inside to make sure.

"Surprise!"

Jules's hand flew to her chest, and her eyes widened. Someone turned on the light to reveal a well-decorated living room, most of her family in Oak Harbor and Noah. Her heart lurched forward, and her lips quivered.

"Don't cry." Noah rushed to her and pulled her into his arms as tears began streaking her face.

"I can't believe you tricked me," she said against his chest.

"I know. I'm sorry. I just didn't want to ruin the surprise," Noah spoke against her hair.

Jules finally raised her head to stare at him. Noah reached up and wiped away the wetness. "How are my two favorite girls doing?"

"Better. Now that you're here," Jules returned.

"Can we start this party now, or do we have to stand here and watch them make googly eyes at each other?"

"Nicki!"

Jules and Noah pulled apart and turned to the others.

"Thank you so much for this, guys. You don't know how happy I am right now," she said, her heart full of gratitude.

"We're happy to do it," Andrea replied with a smile.

"And, Mom, I'm gonna get you back." She turned to her mother with a conspiratorial grin.

"You're welcome," her mother beamed.

Chuckles erupted from the others.

Just like that, her baby shower started on a high note. However, after opening a few presents, she heard Aunt Jo call out in alarm.

"Something's wrong with Mom!"

Jules turned to see her mother and aunts surrounding Becky, whose eyes had rolled to the back of her head until all that could be seen were the whites of her eyes.

Jules felt her heart vacate her body.

"Someone call an ambulance, now!" Cora called out frantically.

Chapter Twenty-Five

Cora paced the small waiting area frantically as she waited for news about her mother. Her sisters sat arm in arm with blank looks, and Uncle Luke and Tessa stood in a corner, speaking in hushed tones and occasionally glancing at her.

Her shoulders were stiff, and her legs felt like lead, but she had to continue moving— walking the length of the small room, or she would go crazy. All she wanted was to find the closest chair to curl up in and cry. Her lips trembled as tears stung her eyes. She bit down on her bottom lip to stifle her sob. The door opened just then, and everyone's gaze turned to it.

Jamie walked through the door, an apologetic look on his face as he probably realized everyone was expecting the doctor to walk through instead. His eyes found Cora, delving deep and offering comfort all at once. Slowly, she walked over to him, and his arms automatically pulled her into a comforting embrace.

"I'm so sorry I didn't get here sooner," he spoke against her hair.

Bittersweet Memories

"You're here now," Cora said into his chest.

The door opened once more, and the doctor walked through it this time. Cora pulled away from Jamie and turned expectantly to the woman, and her sisters rose to their feet. She felt her heart stop for a millisecond at the woman's serious look.

"Doctor, how is she? How is my mother?" Cora's eyes pleaded with the woman to have good news for them.

The woman glanced around the room, her gaze resting on Jamie.

"I'm going to go get you something to drink," Jamie told Cora, who nodded okay. Then he left the room.

The doctor finally turned her gaze to Cora, and her sisters huddled beside her. The woman released a long, heavy sigh, and Cora's anxiety skyrocketed.

"A chest X-ray and blood tests revealed she has pneumonia. We drained the fluid and administered antibiotics intravenously. The fever is down, but she's on a ventilator. She's under observation now."

"Does that mean she'll be all right?" Andrea asked.

"The best we can do now is to make sure that she is comfortable," the woman said, pursing her lips and bringing her eyes down in apology.

Cora stared questioningly back at the short woman before her, as did her sisters, Uncle Luke, his wife, and Tessa. Then, finally, the doctor released another heavy sigh, and her eyes shone with regret.

"I'm sorry, but Becky is in respiratory failure. Once a patient with ALS approaches the final stage of the disease and is diagnosed with pneumonia, there is an eighty-five percent chance they won't survive past a month."

"So, you're saying..." Jo placed her hand over her open mouth, unable to finish the question.

"Mom has less than a month," Cora finished.

193

"I know it isn't the news you were hoping for, but Becky has been strong throughout all of this. My advice, as before, is to spend the remaining time you have making memories," the doctor advised, placing a comforting hand on Cora's arm.

All Cora could manage was to nod her head mechanically. Andrea and Jo collapsed onto the sofa, but Cora remained standing.

"I should also advise you that due to the nature of Becky's illness, it would be best to place her in a hospice care facility where they can monitor her carefully and administer any necessary medical attention. However, you can choose to provide care for her at your home, but that means you'll have to get an around-the-clock nurse."

Cora could hardly raise her head which felt like a canon ball atop her shoulders. "We'll have to discuss this as a family before making a decision," she informed the doctor, who nodded in understanding.

"All right then. I'll give you all some privacy," the doctor responded, leaving the room.

Cora turned to her sisters expectantly, waiting for their input. "What should we do?" she asked.

"I think we should take her home and let her family be there for her," Andrea said.

"I agree," Jo responded with a heavy sigh.

Cora turned to her uncle. "What do you think, Uncle Luke?"

"It's up to you girls to decide what's best for your mother. Samuel isn't here either, but I'm sure he would be proud of your choices and how you handled the situation. You girls are strong, brave, and kind. A product of both your parents."

"Thanks, Uncle." Cora smiled appreciatively.

"Anytime, kiddo." Uncle Luke replied, pulling her into a hug.

Bittersweet Memories

The doctor came back just as they separated. "Have you decided what you will do?" she asked.

"Yes. We will be taking her home," Cora informed the woman.

"Okay, I'll draft the release forms." The woman turned to leave.

"We're going to let the others know what is happening," he told them, reaching for Maria's hand and pulling her toward the door.

Jo looked up at the doctor. "Can we see her?" she asked.

"She's still under observation, but she will be released as soon as the paperwork is finished," she replied. Then, turning back to them, she said, "I know this is a difficult time for all of you but cherish the time you have left with Becky; let her know you are there for her so that her transition can be a peaceful one."

Cora felt a lump form in her throat as she nodded. She looked around at her sisters and noticed that their eyes glistened with unshed tears, but they began to slip down as soon as the door clicked shut.

Cora rushed to them and spread her arms wide to accommodate them both. "We'll get through this. As long as we have each other." Releasing the hug, she took a seat on the couch.

"I just miss her so much already," Jo sobbed. "She is literally living in a lifeless body. I am so... tired... of losing everyone I love." She released a guttural cry and held her head between her palms.

Cora's heart fell at her sister's brokenness. She looked over to Andrea to see her staring unblinkingly ahead as silent tears marred her cheeks and dripped from her chin.

Cora released a shuddering breath. "I know this isn't what we expected when we moved home, and it's hard to see Mom like... this, knowing that she's dying and there's nothing we can do to help her, but I want us to try and focus on the time we have left to show her how much we love her. I want us to remember all the good memories we've shared. Can you do that?" She looked from sister to sister expectantly.

Andrea and Jo nodded, also.

The door opened, and the doctor stepped inside.

"All right, everything is set for Becky to be discharged. You just have a few forms to sign at the receptionist's desk. An ambulance is on standby, and Becky is prepared for the transport."

"Thank you, Doctor. I appreciate your help in all of this," Cora said, mustering a grateful smile.

The doctor bowed her head. "I have a list of healthcare professionals you can use for this final phase," she informed Cora, giving her the paper with the names.

Cora took the paper. "Thank you," she said gratefully. The woman gave her an encouraging nod.

When she left, Cora turned to her sisters. "Ready to go see her?"

Instead of answering, they got up from the sofa and followed her through the door. They walked down the long hallway, and Cora stopped by the front desk. "You can go ahead. I'll fill out the forms and join you," she told them. When they were finally out of sight, her mask slipped, her lips twitched downward, and her eyes filled with sadness.

"Hey."

The soft touch of Jamie's hand on her back and his voice were all it took for her to break down. Cora turned and flew into his arms. Jamie's hand cradled her head against his chest as her tears ran unchecked.

"I'm here... I'm not going anywhere," he affirmed, tightening his arms around her. The warmth emanating from his body was comforting, and his words chipped away at the hollowness threatening to overwhelm her. Cora separated from him when she was spent. She looked up into his warm eyes and smiled through her tears.

"Thank you," she spoke with feeling.

Jamie reached down and intertwined their fingers. Cora looked down at their connected hands before staring back at his smiling face. He reached up with his free hand and used his thumb to wipe away the wetness from her face.

Cora's heart warmed. She was grateful for the tender touch. She didn't realize how much she needed that until now.

"Excuse me, Miss Hamilton."

Cora pulled her gaze from Jamie to look over at the receptionist giving her an apologetic look.

"You need to sign the documents for us to move your mother and the ambulance service," the woman advised.

"Oh, right." She stepped away from Jamie and made her way to the desk. The woman pushed the papers toward her, and Cora spent the next five minutes signing the documents and affixing her signature. Jamie stood only a few feet from her.

"Thank you. Everything seems in order," the receptionist said.

Cora returned her smile and then turned to Jamie. "I'm gonna check on Mom before they move her," she informed him. Jamie inclined his head in understanding.

"I'll meet you in the lobby," he told her.

Cora nodded and turned toward the elevator leading up to the ward her mother was on. When she stepped into the room, her heart lurched forward, threatening to break out of her chest. Andrea and Jo sat on either side of the bed as their mother lay still, eyes closed and several tubes running from her hand, her nose, and from under the hospital gown. Her face was pale and thin, as was the rest of her body; over the months, she'd lost muscle mass. The only sign that she was still alive was the steady beeping of the vital sign machine.

At her approach, Cora's sisters looked at her. Their doleful expressions mirrored the turmoil she felt.

"They said they'll be moving her in the next ten minutes," Andrea spoke. Cora nodded again as she stood over her mother.

She reached down and placed her hand on top of Becky's. Her mother's hand was cold to the touch, as if she was already gone. A tear threatened to fall, but Cora tilted her head back to stop it.

"Mom, we're here. Just... hold on a while longer," she said soft and urgent. Her sisters rose to their feet and came to stand by her. They reached down and placed their hands on to of hers.

"Hold on, Mom," Andrea implored.

A few minutes later, the paramedics entered the room and began strapping Becky down to transport her to the ambulance.

"Can we ride with her?" Jo asked.

"I'm sorry, ladies, but only one relative is allowed in the ambulance," one of the men informed them.

Jo's face fell, and her lips trembled.

"Jo, you can ride with her. We'll meet you back at the house," Cora offered, and Andrea nodded. Their sister flashed them a grin before following the paramedics out. Cora and Andrea made their way to the elevator and rode to the lobby. The minute their family saw them, they came rushing up to them.

"Mom's being transported home by the ambulance. Jo's with her now, and Jules and Noah are back at the house," Cora spoke first. Her eyes found her uncle.

"I already told them about the pneumonia and what the doctor said," he told her. Cora gave him a grateful smile.

After accepting hugs and comfort from their cousins, they separated and headed to their vehicles.

"I'm going to ride with Jamie," Cora informed Andrea, who bobbed her head agreement.

"I'll drive you back, Drea," Kerry said, holding her hand out for the car keys.

"I can drive myself," Andrea gave out.

"I know that, but I insist," Kerry returned with a pointed look. Sighing, Andrea dropped the keys into her cousin's waiting palm, and the two made their way to the car.

Cora turned to see Jamie waiting for her. She walked up to him and followed him to his truck. Jamie opened her door and helped her into the passenger seat before making his way to the driver's side. Jamie started the vehicle and turned on the heat but didn't drive out of the hospital's parking lot. The two sat in silence for more than three minutes. Finally, Cora whimpered, and her tears flowed freely once more. Jamie reached over the dashboard and pulled her into his lap. Cora collapsed against his chest, her forehead resting against his shoulder as she poured out more of her pent-up grief.

Chapter Twenty-Six

"Welcome to childbirth classes. My name is Cleo, and I will be your instructor for the duration of your pregnancy. This is a late-stage class. We will be covering a considerable amount of information in a short time. Before we begin, I'll allow you to introduce yourselves and say how far along in your pregnancy you are."

Jules glanced around the room at the other expectant mothers' bright and eager faces as they sat with their significant others, who looked just as excited or as if they would rather be somewhere else. She tilted her head and rolled her eyes to look at Noah sitting beside her. His passive expression made it difficult for her to gauge his feelings.

"We will start with that couple by the window."

Jules's eyes widened as she realized that the instructor was pointing at her and Noah. Her index finger pointed at her chest in question.

"Yes, you dear." The woman smiled warmly.

Jules turned to see Noah looking back at her with an encouraging tilt of his lips. Then, releasing her breath, she turned to the class. "Hi, my name is Julia, Jules for short," she started. Then, pointing to Noah, she said, "This is Noah, and we are almost nine months pregnant."

"Welcome, Jules and Noah. It's a pleasure to have you here," Cleo greeted warmly. Noah's hand rested on her shoulder, giving her a reassuring squeeze. The instructor continued pointing out the other couples.

"Now that we've all become acquainted, it is time to get into why we came today," Cleo spoke with excitement, her hands clasped before her chest. "Today, we will discuss the signs of labor, pain management, and what to do if the baby is breached. After that, you will practice some breathing exercises with your partner and work on building trust."

The instructor directed them to sit on the cushioned floor, explaining that she needed the mothers to be as comfortable as possible. Noah helped Jules to the floor before sitting beside her. She noted that the other women sat between the legs of their partners. Disappointment settled in her chest, but then Noah reached over and rested his palm on top of hers resting on the floor. Warmth replaced her disappointment. She tried to focus on what the instructor was presenting, but the warm weight on her hand was hard to ignore. She turned her head just in time to see Noah's green eyes staring down at her, his gaze soft and filled with emotion. She felt her heart rate spike.

"All right, now we will practice our breathing exercises," Cleo said, smacking her hands together and effectively thrusting them out of their trance. Jules blinked rapidly as her head turned to the front of the class.

"I need all the males to help your partner get settled on one of these cushions, and then I need you to get in a kneeling position behind her. Females, get as comfortable as you can."

Jules allowed Noah to help her up before settling on the cushion he placed on the floor. She couldn't see Noah anymore but could feel his warmth behind her.

"There are eight positions that we will be learning today that should help ease the pain and discomfort during birth, especially if you won't be taking any pain relievers. The first one is the butterfly pose; this pose elongates the spine and stretches the pelvic floor and your inner thighs."

Jules keenly watched Cleo position herself on the floor, bringing the soles of her feet together, and she widened her legs. As she attempted to follow the pose, she felt Noah's hand on the middle of her back and the other on her shoulder.

"You've got this," he said against her ear. It was all the encouragement she needed to focus on doing it right.

"Excellent, Jules, Noah," Cleo praised as she walked around the room, offering praise and guidance to the couples.

Jules's heart swelled with pride. However, as they progressed through the exercises, there were some that proved difficult for her, and Cleo had to give further directions. Noah was with her all the way offering his own words of encouragement and keeping contact with her, either with a hand on her shoulder, arm, or back.

"All right, class. That's it for today. You all did great. Well done. I look forward to our next class," Cleo said triumphantly.

Noah helped Jules up, and after returning the birthing aides to their right locations, they exited the room.

"That was fun," Noah expressed as they made their way to his car.

"It was," she agreed with a smile.

"Want to get something to eat?"

"Of course. I'm starving," Jules said with an exaggerated sigh.

Noah chuckled as he opened the door for her and helped her settle in her seat.

"So where should we go?" he asked as he cruised along Pioneer Way. Jules was amazed at how quaint and vibrant downtown Oak Harbor was. Small, conjoined shops painted in homely shades with white awnings took up entire blocks. They were family run, with many catering to collectors of antiques. Malls, high-rise office buildings, and car lots were dispersed throughout the town. The smell of the salty ocean air carried on the wind was indicative of the nearness of the ocean as the town was nestled at the water's edge.

"Let's try a seafood joint," she suggested. "I'm craving crab legs and tartar sauce."

"All right," Noah concurred , turning the car onto Maui Ave. Two minutes later, they pulled into the parking lot at Seaside Hideaway. The two alighted from the car and made their way toward the establishment's front door.

"Hi, welcome to Seaside Hideaway, the number one seafood restaurant in all of Whidbey. My name is Carly."

Jules beamed at the young woman with hair the color of wheat and a bright smile that lit up her whole face as she stood before them in a logoed polo shirt and black slacks.

"Hi, Carly. We'd like a table for two, please," Noah said.

"Of course, follow me," Carly chirped. She led them to a table at the far corner, closest to the large bay windows offering the perfect view of the outdoor dining area and the beautiful blue-green water of the bay.

"These are your menus. I'll go get a jug of ice water for you, and hopefully, you'll be ready to order when I get back," Carly informed them as she placed the black and white menus in their hands.

"Thank you." Jules smiled.

"There are a lot of choices on this menu. Are you still sticking to crab legs?" Noah inquired, perusing the menu after Carly left.

"I'm sure I want them." She chuckled. "I'm going to add some lobster tails, garlic bread, mashed potatoes, and key lime pie for dessert."

Noah's eyes widened, and his jaw dropped open.

"What?" Jules laughed. "I'm eating for two, you know?"

"I know, but that is still a lot of food. Are you sure you will be able to handle it?"

Jules tapped her index against her chin in thought. "Good point. Maybe I'll just do the garlic bread and forego the potatoes," she conceded.

It was Noah's time to chuckle. His green eyes shone with admiration as he stared at her. "Sometimes you amaze me, Jules."

She felt her cheeks get warm, and she quickly ducked her head.

"Are you folks ready to order?" Carly appeared with the jug of water and poured them each a glass.

"Yes," Noah responded. "I'll have your seafood boil and a Sprite," Noah ordered.

"And I'll have the king crab legs, a serving of lobster tails, garlic bread, and your key lime pie for dessert," Jules requested.

"Okay, coming right up," Carly said, shutting the small book she wrote their order in.

After Carly left, Noah turned to Jules. "How are you feeling?"

"Pretty good," Jules answered truthfully.

Noah nodded, but his gaze remained fixed on her. Their green depths probed, and Jules had to sink her short nails into her palms not to squirm under his gaze.

"How are you feeling?" he repeated.

Jules opened her mouth to reply as before but snapped it shut as she really thought about it. Her shoulders sagged as she released a heavy breath. "I'm scared," she breathed barely above a whisper. "My grandmother is on the brink of death, and I'm about to bring a new life into this world." Jules looked over at Noah with eyes gutted with pain. "I'm terrified," her voice trembled.

Noah's palm landed on her hand, resting on the table. Jules looked down at their connected hands before looking at him.

"I can't imagine how hard this must be for you witnessing your grandmother dying slowly. I didn't get to say goodbye to my grandad, and it tears at my heart every day, but you got to spend time with your grandmother. Cherish the memories you shared and spend time to let her know how much you appreciate her."

Jules's eyes watered. "But it's so hard...I just got to know her, and now I'm losing her," she whimpered.

Noah's eyes filled with understanding. "I know."

"All right, here you go." Noah released Jules's hand and sat back in his seat as their waitress announced her presence. "Seafood boil for you, crab legs, lobster tails, and garlic bread for you." She placed their meals before them. "Enjoy," she encouraged with a bright smile.

Jules managed to grin just a little.

After Carly left, Jules turned to Noah, who was already looking at her. "I know words aren't enough, but it will get better, and you will make a wonderful mother."

Jules gave him a grateful look.

"Okay, we've shared a lot of heavy topics; let's enjoy this splendid food— it smells delicious, by the way." He averted his gaze to look at the food.

Jules looked down at her food and began to salivate. "I couldn't agree with you more," she said, reaching for a crab leg. Using her hand, she cracked the hard exterior hiding the sweet meat in its calcified cocoon. She dipped the exposed flesh in the tartar sauce and brought it to her lips.

"Mhmm." She sighed.

"That good, huh?" Noah asked, his eyes filled with glee.

Jules eagerly nodded and further dug into her food, enjoying the juicy, buttery, fresh crab and lobster meat. Next,

Noah turned his attention to his meal, and as he dug into it, he gestured his approval.

"That was some good seafood," Jules complimented as they walked along the marina boardwalk, enjoying the scenery of the vessels moored along the docs, the contrast of light blue sky and the dark blue waters creating the magnificent backdrop to the sea of white.

"The food was great," Noah agreed.

Sitting at one of the picnic tables, the two stared out at the water, absorbing the serenity of it all. Jules noticed Noah reach for something in his pocket from the corner of her eye. She turned to see him staring at his cell phone vibrating in his hand with a deep crease between his brows. He ended the call, put the phone back in his pocket, and looked out at the water again. However, a minute later, his cell vibrated. Like before, he glanced at the screen and ended the call. His cell rang almost instantaneously after that.

"You know you can answer the call. I don't mind," she advised him.

"It's fine," Noah replied.

Jules's brows furrowed. "Obviously, it must be important if the person keeps calling back." Just then, his cell rang, but he didn't answer it. Jules narrowed her eyes. "Who is it?"

"It's no one."

"Noah. Who is it?" Jules pressed.

After a short pause, Noah released a heavy breath. "It's Dina," he confessed.

Jules's brows lifted to her hairline. "Your ex?"

Noah's head tipped forward, and Jules sucked in her breath. Just then, his phone vibrated.

"Answer it," she instructed, steel in her voice. Noah hesitated. "You gave her your number, so surely you knew she would call."

"My mom gave her my number," he corrected, finally

touching the answer button and placing the phone against his ear. "Hello?"

Jules turned her head to look out at the calm waters, but a tumultuous storm brewed in her mind. "What did she want?" she asked when he ended the call.

Noah looked over her, but Jules kept her gaze forward. He sighed. "She wants us to talk to try and work things out."

There was a long uncomfortable silence before Jules finally spoke. "It's obvious you still have feelings for her."

"That's not—"

Jules's hand came up, silencing him.

"I was willing to try this whole relationship with you, but I can't... not until I am sure you are fully there. You need to figure out what you want, Noah, and you need to set your mother straight about why you two broke up." She turned to him this time, her blue eyes determined. "I won't play second fiddle to your ex just because she was your first love."

"Jules, please, I—"

"Can you take me home?"

The two traveled in silence, each lost in their thoughts. When they made it to the house, Jules exited the car and instructed him not to follow. Noah stayed until she disappeared into the house.

Jules bypassed the kitchen, where she heard her mother and aunts talking, and went straight to her room. She flopped on her bed, feeling miserable. *Why did everything have to be so complicated?* Life kept changing, wrestling control away from her. It was frightening. She just wanted some stability in her life, something familiar.

She reached for her phone and dialed the one person she vowed she wouldn't call.

"Hello? Jules, is that you?" the voice on the other end of the line asked with surprise.

"Yeah, Dad, it's me."

Chapter Twenty-Seven

Cora sat by her mother's bedside, watching the rise and fall of her chest as she slept. The vitals machine beeped steadily, confirming that Becky was still present in an otherwise lifeless body.

She reached over to brush away a few strands of her thin, gray hair from her face.

Her thin, sallow face was cold to the touch.

Cora got up and went to turn up the thermostat before posting herself by her mother's bedside once more.

"Hi, Mom. It's me, Cora. I never thought a day like this would come so soon, but here it is upon us." Cora paused as tears pooled in her eyes, a few breaking free to create a stained path down her cheek. She swallowed the lump in her throat as she struggled to speak. "I'm sorry I left home for so long. I wish I had stayed or at least tried harder to stay in contact with you. Maybe it would have made the thought of losing you so soon more bearable." Cora chuckled through her tears. "Who am I kidding? There is nothing that could ever make the thought of losing you more bearable." She gulped back a sob. "I know it's selfish, though, to keep you here just because I don't want to lose you, knowing that you're suffering." She cupped her mother's cheek. "What gives me comfort is knowing that Dad is waiting for you on the other side, with a bouquet of roses, no doubt." She snickered, then sobered up. "I know that when you finally leave us, you will be leaving all this pain behind and that you will be free."

Cora stood to her feet, leaned forward, and kissed her mother's forehead. "I promise I will keep you in my heart and your memory alive for as long as I live," she lovingly whispered close to her mother's ear. Then, she turned and left the room. Cora leaned against the closed door as tears rolled down her face. She quickly swiped her face with the back of her hand at the approaching footsteps.

"Mom, are you okay?" Jules asked, coming to a stop beside her.

"I am, sweetie," Cora returned.

Jules's blue eyes probed. "Are you sure?"

Cora was tempted to repeat that she was fine, but at her daughter's look of worry, she confessed, "I was just talking to Mom, and it made me a little sad."

"Oh, Mom." Jules sighed. She looked from Cora to Becky's closed door. "I wish there was some way to make her better. I hate this." Her lips turned down into a sad frown.

"Me too, sweetie," Cora agreed, pulling her daughter to her and hugging her shoulders. Jules's rested her head against her mother's chest and slid her arms around her back.

"Would you like some hot chocolate? I'm on my way to the kitchen," Cora offered when they separated.

Jules nodded. The two made their way to the kitchen, and Cora put on the kettle and then pulled down two mugs from the cupboard. After adding the instant cocoa mix, she poured the hot water and added milk before stirring. She placed the steaming hot cup before her daughter and sat across from her with her cup. Jules took a sip from her cup and gestured her approval.

"How are you?" Cora asked.

"Noah got a call from his ex-girlfriend. She wants to get back together."

Cora noticed the tick in Jules's jaw. "What did Noah say?"

Jules released a frustrated breath. "It doesn't matter what he says. His ex should not have access to him like that. He did say it was his mother who gave her the number, but that just makes it worse. His family approves of her and not me, and he won't tell them what she did," she vented.

Cora stared at her daughter with compassion. "Jules, that man loves you," she clearly stated, causing her daughter to look at her wide-eyed. "His ex is a mere distraction. You must give him time to sort things out with her and his mother. You also need to allow him to talk and express himself." Cora's head sliced to the side sharply, stopping her daughter from speaking.

"I know you, Jules. You can be hard-headed and unwilling to listen." She leaned forward and touched Jules's arm as she stared at her thoughtfully. "Give him a chance."

Jules cut her gaze away from Cora. She eventually sighed again and said, "Okay. I'll... try."

Cora looked pleased.

"I called Dad last night."

"You did?" Cora's eyes widened in surprise. Jules nodded.

"How did that go?" she asked.

Jules brought the hot mug to her lips and took another sip of her hot beverage before replying. "It was liberating," she said, putting her cup down on the island and staring at her mother. "I expressed how I've felt about him for the past two years after what he did to our family, and then I told him that I forgave him."

Cora stared at her daughter. "I am so proud of you."

Jules smiled appreciatively. Cora washed the dirty cups

and put them away after they were finished. She bid her daughter goodnight, and Jules headed for her room. Cora sat on the front porch to wait for the night nurse for her mother.

* * *

"Look who's here," Andrea burst through the back door, stepping onto the wraparound porch, and said excitedly. She stepped aside to reveal her daughter Rory and her husband, James.

"Oh my, Rory. We're so glad to have you back," Cora beamed as she rose from her seat to hug her niece. "And you, too, James." She turned to embrace the young man.

"Hi, Cora. It is good to see you too," James greeted politely.

"Hi, Rory. Hi, James." Jules waved from the rocking chair she sat in.

"Hi, Jules," Rory said. "I'm glad I came back in time to witness the birth." She grinned, jutting her chin out and gesturing to Jules's swollen belly.

"I'm glad too," Jules returned. A moment passed between them that didn't go unnoticed by Cora. She remembered that they had bonded back in November when Rory was preparing for her wedding on the island. She was happy Jules connected with her cousin, as they hadn't grown up together.

"Where's Aunt Jo?" Rory asked, looking around.

"She's at the restaurant," Cora replied.

"Okay, I'll go see her a little later."

"So, how was Africa?" Cora asked as everyone settled on a chair.

"It was wonderful," Rory praised. "We got to experience so many wonderful things, and the Safari excursions were just magnificent."

"It was scorching hot too," James added, causing everyone to chuckle.

"It did you two well. Do you see how tan they are?" Andrea directed at Cora.

"What are your plans now that you're back?" Cora asked.

"We're renting a house close by, on Torpedo Drive, until we can find a house to buy. James starts working at the law firm with Ethan in two weeks, and I'm waiting to hear back from the elementary school," Rory expressed.

"That's wonderful, dear. It seems you two have everything worked out." Cora bowed her head in approval. "I'm sure you'll be hearing from the school soon."

"I hope so too," Rory expressed. "I'll have some time on my hands until then. I just wish I had been here to have some time with Grandma before..." she trailed off as her lips turned down into a sad frown.

"Don't beat yourself up, sweetie. This disease is more than what we had anticipated it would be. Mom cannot speak to you, but you can talk to her. She'll hear you," Cora encouraged.

Rory nodded, but sadness still clouded her light green eyes.

* * *

"Jules, Noah is here to see you."

"Now?" Jules asked, looking up at her mother.

Cora inclined her head and stepped away from the door to reveal Noah.

"Hi," he said with a slight wave.

"Hi," she returned.

"I'll give you two some privacy." Cora turned and left.

"Would you like a seat?" she asked, moving over on the sofa to provide room.

"Um, no, I can't," he declined.

Jules stared at him in confusion.

"I was hoping we could go for a walk," he explained.

"Oh. Okay," she replied simply.

Jules followed Noah down the back porch steps a few minutes later. They walked along the cobbled stone path leading toward the dock. Jules threw furtive glances at him, but she didn't say anything. For the past week, they had been going to their birthing classes, but their interaction with each other had been stiff and awkward compared to their first class. She'd had her second to last gynecologist visit, and her doctor had mentioned that she was picking up a negative vibe between them which they denied.

"I talked to Dina."

Jules's head snapped up.

Noah looked over at her before he stared ahead as they continued walking. "I told her there was no future for us and that she shouldn't call me again. Then, I told my mother what she had done. She was so mad. She was also sorry for the way she treated you."

Jules's mouth opened in surprise, but no words came. Then, finally, they stopped by the dock, and Noah turned and held her hands in his.

"I thought I loved Dina because we grew up together, went to school together, and it made sense at the time. But what we shared was puppy love. It took her cheating for me to realize that. I'm telling you this because I never got butterflies just by thinking about her. She didn't make my heart leap by just looking at me. But, you, Jules, I find my heart beats a million miles a minute, and I always have butterflies when I am around you. I love you, Jules, more than I ever knew was possible. I'm not just saying this because you are the mother of my child, but since the first day I saw you back in Seoul, I knew I would marry you one day. I just hope you'll be able to accept me, flaws and all," Noah implored.

Jules's heart felt as if it would burst out of her chest as she listened to him.

"I want to spend the rest of my life showing you how much

I love you. I want us to be a family. So, I found a house nearby and signed a lease because it doesn't matter where we live as long as we're together and get to be a family."

Jules threw her hands over his shoulders and kissed whatever he was about to say away.

"I love you too, Noah McKinley," she professed after their lips separated. "I can't wait for us to be a family." The baby kicked just then as if in agreement.

Noah's bright green eyes shone with so much emotion as he scooted Jules up into his arms and kissed her again. "I love you," he breathed against her lips.

Jules didn't think she would ever get tired of hearing him say it, bringing a brilliant smile to her lips. "I love you."

"I planned something special for us," he said, leading her by her hand up the dock.

"More special than your profession of love?" Jules asked.

"Of course not." Noah chuckled. "It's the icing on the cake."

Coming up to the *Silver Bullet*, safely moored and lightly rocking with the soft movement of the water, Jules stared questioningly at him. Noah helped her down and joined her.

"Your mother permitted us to take her out on the water and have a wonderful afternoon."

Jules laughed and shook her head, realizing that her mother was their biggest supporter. Jules looked around, taking in the picnic basket and a thick blanket at the back of the boat.

"Oh, champagne." She smiled, holding up the bottle of bubbly.

"Nonalcoholic." Noah chuckled as he started the engine, lightly revving it as the vessel slowly pulled away from the doc. Jules held her face to the sun, enjoying the light rays and the slight heat to combat the crisp air around them as the boat sliced through the pristine blue waters.

She took the time to enjoy the mountain ranges suspended

Bittersweet Memories

in the distance. Noah cut the engine sometime later and spread the blanket on the boat's deck before laying out the items in the picnic basket.

"Everything looks so delicious," she drooled. Noah held out his hand to help her up. She felt a sudden stab of pain at her side that caused her to wince.

"Are you okay?" Noah asked in concern.

"Yeah, I just felt a bit of pain just now," she expressed. Then, she felt another stabbing pain that caused her to bowl over, holding her stomach. Her eyes widened when she felt something wet trickle down her leg. She looked up at Noah with alarm.

"My water just broke."

"What? Right now?" he asked stupidly.

"Yes, right... no— AH!" Jules cried out as another contraction ripped through her abdomen.

This seemed to thrust Noah into action. "All right, just breathe. Remember what Cleo taught you, hee-hee-hoo," Noah mimicked the instructor. If Jules wasn't feeling so much pain, she would have laughed.

At the sign of another contraction, Jules tried to do the exercise. "Hee-hee-hoooo—AH. This isn't helping!" she cried, tightly holding the hand Noah gave her. He slowly lowered her to the seat before heading back to the deck for the blanket.

"I'm going to spread this down here and put you on it to minimize the impact of the boat hitting the waves. I have to get you back to shore now. Your contractions are too close, which means this baby is ready to pop out at any minute." Noah lowered her onto the blanket and made his way to the helm, and sped to shore.

"AH! Noah, I-I-I can't..."

"We're almost there. Just hold on," Noah called back.

Sweat washed over her face, and she bit down on her lip to stop the scream threatening to escape her lips. She tightly wound the blanket around her hands as she prayed for them to make it back.

Noah almost crashed the boat against the dock in his frantic dash to get Jules safely back to the mainland. Quickly securing the boat, he helped Jules out before gathering her in his arms and taking off for the house.

Jules shut her eyes and wound her arms around Noah's neck. At the sound of sirens, her eyes flew open, and she glanced up at Noah, who looked just as surprised. Surely, they hadn't anticipated that she was going into labor and called an ambulance for her. Her heart clunked to the bottom of her chest as the realization hit her.

Noah burst through the back door and marched down the hall. His steps faltered when an EMT wheeled Becky out of her room. Jules gasped in surprise at her grandmother's unmoving body, an unusual bluish hue to her skin. Cora walked out just then, tears soaking her face and blouse.

Ignoring her pain, Jules called out, "Mom."

Cora's head snapped in their direction, her eyes widening with surprise and concern.

"What happened?" she asked.

"Jules's water broke," Noah answered.

Cora's hand flew to her lips in alarm.

"What's wrong with Grandma?" Jules asked, trying to look at Becky.

Cora hesitated for a second before responding. "Mom's breathing has been further impacted, and she has been unresponsive. She needs to get to the hospital as soon as possible."

"Ma'am, we need to know who will be riding with your mother," the EMT interrupted.

"Can my daughter travel in the ambulance? She's in labor," Cora informed the man.

The EMT's brows furrowed as she looked from her to Jules, then back at her. "How far along are the contractions?"

"Very close, about five to ten minutes apart," Noah responded urgently.

The man hesitated for a moment. "All right, there's a small stretcher in the back. I'll get it for your daughter, but that means only she and your mother can travel in the ambulance."

"That's fine," Cora hurriedly replied.

The EMT wheeled Becky out to the ambulance, and Noah followed with Jules still in his arms.

Chapter Twenty-Eight

"Oh my god, it hurts," Jules whimpered as the contractions became more intense. It felt as if someone had taken a knife and ripped her stomach apart. She gripped the corners of the flat, cushioned table she was lying on as the ambulance sailed down the highway to the hospital.

"Just hold on a few more minutes, miss. We're almost at the hospital. They're already waiting for you when we get there," a female EMT sitting on one of the bolted-down seats to her side explained. "Unless you want your baby to be delivered here," she added.

Jules quickly shook her head. A wave of nausea swept over her with the next contraction, but she quickly gulped it down and tried to use her breathing exercise to settle her stomach and make the pain more bearable. Her eyes watered from the excruciating pain and because her grandmother lay on the other stretcher across her, knocking on death's door.

She used her remaining strength to reach for her grandmother. Becky's face felt cold to the touch. Jules whimpered at the realization that her grandmother was indeed close to death. The machines beeping above her head were the only indication that she was still in the land of the living.

"Grandma, if you can hear me, please...hold on," she pleaded. Her hand fell away when the ambulance stopped, and someone opened the door. The EMTs wheeled them toward the waiting health officials at the A&E department.

"Julia Avlon, twenty-two, went into labor over forty-five minutes ago; contractions are now five minutes apart," the EMT informed the waiting nurse and attendee as they transferred Jules to a wheelchair.

"All right, we'll take it from here," the nurse replied. "The delivery room is already prepped, and her doctor will be here shortly." They wheeled her into the lobby. "I just need to get a few papers, then we can go," the nurse said, and the lady at the desk handed her some sheets of paper.

"Wait, my grandmother," Jules said frantically, holding her hand toward her grandmother, who was being wheeled away.

"They're taking your grandmother to another wing of the hospital. Don't worry, dear; she'll be okay." The nurse smiled reassuringly down at her.

Jules's face fell, and her upper lip trembled as she watched Becky move further and further away from her. Tears streamed down her face.

"Jules, I'm here." Noah stopped before her with her hospital bag and was out of breath. She looked up at him and broke down even more.

"Hey, hey, what's wrong?" he asked, kneeling before the wheelchair. He used his thumb to wipe a few of her tears and caress her cheek lovingly.

"I want my mom," she sobbed.

"Cora will be here shortly. She went with your aunts to check on Becky," Noah said. Then, using the hand resting on her cheek and under her chin, he turned her face so that she was looking at him. "Everything will be okay," he encouraged. "Do you trust me?" he probed.

Jules nodded.

"For the next hour, I need you to focus only on giving birth. Our daughter needs you, Jules. Nothing else matters," he insisted.

"All right," Jules said through her tears.

"I'm sorry, but we need to get her to the delivery room now," the nurse informed Noah. He stepped back and allowed them to push Jules toward the elevator.

Jules looked back at him with question and fear in her eyes.

"I'll be there shortly." Noah smiled as the elevator doors slid shut. A few minutes later, Jules was situated in a private room, and her sundress was being swapped for a hospital gown. She then lay on the bed in a half-sitting position, her back being supported by pillows.

"Hello, Jules. I came as soon as I heard. How are you feeling?" Her doctor rushed into the room in scrubs and slapping on gloves.

"Honestly?" Jules asked as the sweat pearled on her forehead and her lower half, producing enough pain to numb any other feeling.

The doctor grinned knowingly. "On a scale of one to ten, how bad is the pain?" she asked.

"One hundred," Jules deadpanned. This earned a chuckle from the room.

"I understand, Jules. However, you're not dilated enough for us to go in, but you have been doing wonderful so far," the doctor expressed.

Jules bit down on her bottom lip as another contraction hit her. "Where's Noah?" she asked after the pain subsided. She glanced around the room, but none of the faces staring back at her was Noah.

"I'm here," Noah said, walking over to Jules and taking her

hand. Relief washed over her as she looked into his beaming green eyes.

"Wonderful, now that the father is here, we can begin," her doctor said, coming to stand at her bedside. "Okay, Jules, while we wait for you to become fully dilated, let's practice your breathing."

Jules nodded her agreement and began to do it. Ten minutes later, she reached full dilation and couldn't help but push.

"You're doing great, Jules. You're doing just... great," Noah complimented as he leaned over her and watched. With each new contraction, she squeezed his hand so hard that she heard his intake of breath.

"All right, we're seeing the head. Jules, I need you to make another big push with everything you have." Her doctor looked up at her.

Jules nodded, too tired to respond with words. Noah squeezed her hand in encouragement. She wanted to stop, to give up, but that wasn't an option and would prove dangerous for her and the baby.

"You've got this, Jules," Noah said against her ear.

Sucking in her breath, she pushed. "Ahhh!"

"Congratulations, your daughter is here," the doctor said. Jules collapsed against the pillows, exhausted. Tears mingled with the sweat on her face as she watched the doctor lift up her daughter and Noah cut the umbilical cord.

"You did it," Noah said proudly, kissing her temple in congratulations.

The sound of their baby's first cry brought more tears to Jules's eyes, and when they wrapped her in a towel and put her in Jules's arms, she broke down again, marveling at the little human being that had been inside her.

Her daughter opened her eyes and looked up at Jules, the dark orbs shaped like her father's. Noah reached over and brushed his hand lightly against her face, across her shoulders before nudging her tiny hand with one of his fingers. Jules smiled at the awe on his face.

They took the baby away to check her vitals, clean and weigh her.

"I can't believe we made a little person," Noah remarked. He looked at Jules with admiration. "She's beautiful and perfect, just like her mother.

A smile graced her lips at the compliment.

"Thank you." Noah kissed her. Jules eagerly welcomed the adoration. The nurse brought back the baby, now clothed in a small onesie and swaddled in a blanket. Jules brought the baby to her chest to feed her.

The door opened to reveal her mother and aunts filing into the room with smiling faces.

"Where's my granddaughter? I am dying to meet her," Cora spoke in eagerness.

Jules held out her daughter to Cora, who enthusiastically accepted her. "Oh, look at her little fingers and toes," Cora marveled, rocking her granddaughter.

"How is Grandma?" Jules asked the pressing question that was on her mind.

Cora looked at her with a sad smile before glancing at her sisters behind her. They all wore the same expression that tore at her heart at the revelation that her grandmother was really gone.

***

"Becky was a remarkable woman. She had a light inside her that drew you to her instantly. To know her was to love her."

Cora nodded in agreement with her uncle's statement as he stood at the podium, giving his remembrance of their mother lying in the coffin before them. It stung to know that her

Bittersweet Memories

mother was gone, but she was relieved that Becky was no longer suffering. If nothing else, she was grateful for that. A tear slid down her cheek. She looked over at her sisters, who sat stiffly beside her. The dark shades they wore, like her, hid their red, puffy eyes and tear-streaked faces.

She turned back to her uncle as he continued to speak.

"I remember when my brother fell in love with Becky. He was like a love-sick puppy. He would ask me to help him write love notes to her because I had a way with words he said. Plus, I was already married at the time. Although it did get me in trouble with the miss's as she found the notebook full of love letters and thought I was getting sweet on someone else. I was in the doghouse for many moons." His statement earned a few chuckles from the congregants.

"In Becky, Sam could never have asked for a better partner. She complemented him in every way and instantly fell in love with his family, who, in turn, became in love with her."

Luke grinned. "Becky will be missed, but let us choose to honor her legacy."

Cora's palms came together to applaud her uncle as everyone else did.

"We will now have the eulogy from Rebecca's daughters," the moderator spoke. Rising from their seat, the sisters made their way to the front of the room.

"Hello, everyone," Cora began, looking out at her family and the other people who were in attendance because they knew her mother. She held the waists of her sisters and brought them close to her side for support. "Andrea, Jo, and I are grateful for your support today in remembering our mother's life as the kind, brave, and loving woman she was."

Drawing a deep breath, Cora began, "Rebecca Elizabeth Hamilton was born on May twenty-fifth, 1948..."

Cora and her sisters took their seats when she was finished, and the preacher came and made his closing remarks. The congregants then went to the cemetery where the body would be interred.

Jo collapsed as the casket was being lowered into the earth, but Daniel had been standing behind her to catch her. Donny held Andrea against his chest as she sobbed. Cora also noted that Jules and Erin were clinging to each as Noah held on to their newborn baby. Cora felt someone hold her hand, and she looked up to see Jamie giving her a look of reassurance. She smiled at him before resting her head on his shoulders as she watched the men start to cover Becky. A tear slipped down her face.

"Goodbye, Mom," she whispered before she could no longer see her mother's coffin. Everyone then turned to leave. Jamie drove her home.

"How are you feeling?" Jamie asked after a few minutes of silence. The rain had started to fall, and she had rested her head against the window, watching the water cascade down the glass.

Raising her head, she turned to look at Jamie with a small uplifting of her lips. "I am sad, but I'm glad you're here with me."

Jamie looked at her lovingly, then reached over to clasp her hand with his. "I will always be there for you, Cora. I love you," he spoke sincerely.

Her smile brightened.

"Your mother was a very wonderful woman. She will be greatly missed," an older woman grasped Cora's hand as she spoke back at the house.

"Thank you," she said politely to the woman.

Visitors poured in and out of the house, offering their words of condolence. When they finally left, the family gathered in the living room for a special remembrance that Cora, Andrea, and Jo had put together for their mom.

Andrea slipped the disk into the DVD player, and images

Bittersweet Memories

of Becky popped up on the widescreen, her favorite song playing in the background. There were images of Becky as a baby, images of her as a child, preteen, and teen to adulthood. There were images of her in her bridal gown and Samuel standing beside her, both brightly beaming at the camera. Images of each of the girls after their births with a tired but smiling Becky also popped onto the screen.

Cora grinned through her tears.

Next came pictures and videos of them since moving back to Oak Harbor. Finally, there was a video of them in her room on New Year's Eve, providing her with the beautiful portrait of her.

This made Cora's heart swell with happiness as she recalled how content Becky had been, even though she couldn't say anything. The video then switched to them being at the art museum back in Seattle. She looked over at her sisters, and even though their faces were tear-stained, they were smiling, possibly remembering how much fun they'd had that day.

Cora sighed with satisfaction as she rested her head against Jamie's shoulder. Her family would miss Becky a lot, but she was confident they would all learn to live on with her smiling down on them from up above. The smiling faces were proof of that.

They would all be fine.

Epilogue

One Month Later

"Jules, come on. We have to get to the church on time for Rebecca's christening. It's in..." Noah looked at his watch before looking up at Jules. "0900 hours," he finished.

Jules looked over at the bedside clock. "Noah, it's only eight-fifteen a.m. The church is literally only ten minutes away. Relax," she advised him. "And would you stop with the army time? You should be in civilian mode for the rest of the year."

Noah looked back at Jules, unimpressed.

"Your father is such a worrywart, isn't he?" Jules gently tickled her daughter, receiving a toothless grin as she looked up at her. "Who's the most adorable baby in the world? You are, yes you are," she doted, lifting baby Rebecca into her arms, and rocking her to and fro. She gently kissed Rebecca's dark hair and stared into her eyes. "You are my miracle," she said, a soft smile turning up her lips.

"Okay, we can go," she said, turning to Noah. She sucked in a surprised breath at the intense stare. Noah strode across the room and crashed his lips against hers. "What was that for?" she asked giddily against his lips.

"That was for loving me and for making me the happiest man alive by making me a father," he said between kisses. Jules giggled as his arms came around to cradle her and their daughter. "I love you," he breathed against her lips.

"I love you too." Jules grinned at him. The baby fussing caught their attention, and they both looked down at her.

"You want your kisses too, don't you, my little sun?" Noah reached down and scooped Rebecca out of Jules's hands. A smile instantly brightened her face as he peppered her face with kisses.

Jules stood back, warmed by the scene. Noah was a natural at this. As she watched him dote on their daughter, she couldn't imagine having children with anyone else.

"Ready to go?" Noah asked after Rebecca settled down.

Jules nodded. She reached for the baby bag on the rocking chair and followed Noah down the stairs and out the front door. Ten minutes later, they were ushered into a seat at the front of the church, where their family was already waiting.

"Hi, Mom," she greeted Cora with a kiss to her cheek. "Evelyn, it's so nice to see you," she greeted Noah's mom after with a hug.

"I wouldn't miss my granddaughter's christening for the world," Evelyn said. "And here she is now," she said, looking behind Jules.

"Hi, Mom," Noah said to his mother.

"Can I?" Evelyn asked, holding out her hands to him. Noah gently placed Rebecca into her hands, and Jules smiled at the softening of Evelyn's face as she looked lovingly at her granddaughter. "Look how cute you are," she cooed.

The family settled as the sermon began. An hour later, Jules, Noah, and their family stood at the front of the church as the christening rites were done.

Rebecca was an angel and looked the part in the long white christening gown and white headband she wore. However, when the priest scooped a handful of water over her hair by the cistern, she utilized her lungs to their total capacity, showing her displeasure at getting wet.

They left the church and made their way back to her grandparents' house, which now belonged to her mother and aunts.

The smell of rich, sweet smoke filled Jules's nostrils as she stepped out of the car. Her belly rumbled in anticipation of the feast to come. "Mhmm, I can't wait to taste what Uncle Luke is grilling around back," she said.

Noah chuckled. "Even after such a big breakfast, you're still thinking about food. Admit it; you're a foodie," he teased.

"So, eating good food is a job I'd love to have. So what? I will not have you mock my special talents, young man," Jules lectured, her blue eyes glinting with mischief.

"I'm sorry, Miss Avlon. I will never make fun of any of your hobbies. They're all quite cute, actually," Noah said before her with an equally mischievous glint. He inched closer to her until there was only a hair's breadth between them.

"All right, knock it off you two, or have you forgotten how you got baby number one?"

Jules and Noah backed away from each other, blushing as if they had been caught doing something wrong. She turned to see her sister walking toward them with a wide grin.

"Erin!" Jules squealed, running toward her sister, whose arms were spread wide to receive her as Jules crashed into her.

"I thought you weren't coming," Jules said after they parted.

Erin tried her best to keep her smile, but it slowly fell. "I wasn't sure I would have been able to make it either," she confessed. Her eyes became distant, but as soon as it came, it went.

"Where's that niece of mine that I haven't seen since Grandma's... funeral." The atmosphere dropped a notch, but Noah stepped in just then.

"Hi, Erin. It's nice to see you again," Noah greeted.

"Hi, Noah. It's good to see you," Erin greeted back as he offered her a side hug. "Where's my little niece, by the way?" she asked, looking around as if she would magically appear.

"She's with Mom and Noah's mother. Jamie's driving them. They should be here any minute now," Jules informed her. Erin nodded. "Shall we?" Jules gestured to the porch. They followed her up where other family members walked around the house, either going into the kitchen or taking food outside.

Jules made her way toward the back door and stepped onto the porch. "Hey, kids." Uncle Luke raised his hand in greeting from the grill where he posted himself. Jules and the others waved their greetings.

She walked down the few steps and welcomed the others that were there. "How did the christening go?" Kerry asked, kissing Jules on the cheek.

"It was great," Jules replied.

"And Rebecca was an angel like always, I imagine."

"Almost." Jules chuckled. "She cried when the water touched her head."

"But she loves water," Kerry stated.

"I know. Maybe, it was just because it was a long ceremony," she surmised.

"Let me show you the cakes," Kerry invited.

Jules followed her toward the long marble table under the pergola where other items of food were on display, but the cakes were in the middle of the table on stands. She smiled widely at the beauty and detail of them. "These are great! Thank you," she said gratefully to Kerry. Just then, the others arrived, and all eyes were turned toward Rebecca.

Jules pouted as she watched them dote on her daughter, monopolizing her. "Relax," Noah said from behind her. His hands came up to massage her shoulders. "Let them have their time with her. Tonight, she'll be all ours," he assured her.

"But I just miss holding her," she whined. Noah chuckled, the vibration of it moving through her body.

"Would my fair maiden like me to go rescue our daughter from her aunts and cousins?" he asked.

Jules looked over at her daughter in Erin's hands as Diane, Rory, and Tracey surrounded her, the smiles on their faces indicative of how enraptured they were by her.

Her eyes flickered to the porch to see her father standing there with his hands in his pockets as he rocked on the balls of his feet.

"I think someone else needs rescuing at this time." She pointed at her father.

"Let's go rescue him then," he said, taking her hand. They walked toward Joel.

"Hi, Dad," Jules greeted him with a grin.

"Hi, sweetie," he said, looking down at her. He walked down the steps to join them.

"I'm happy you made it," she spoke with sincerity.

"I'm happy you invited me," he returned with a grateful smile.

Jules took him over toward the rest of the family. She noticed Erin's shocked face that transformed into anger in a split second at his presence. She handed the baby to Diane and walked off. Joel watched her go, his eyes filled with regret.

"Give her time, Dad. She's going through a lot right now. She'll reach out when she's ready," Jules said, placing an encouraging hand on his arm.

Bittersweet Memories

"All right, everyone. Let's gather by this scrumptious meal prepared for all of us," Ben, Aunt Stacey's son, called out.

Everyone moved toward the table. Jules collected Rebecca and sat around the table. Conversation flowed as they dug into the food.

"Attention, everyone," Uncle Luke called out as he stood to his feet. "I stand here looking at all of you, and I must say I could never be prouder of being a member of this family. Through happiness, sadness, through adversities, we have always stood together. I want to encourage you all to keep this spirit alive, even after we, the older ones, are gone," he said, looking at his wife and Aunt Stacy before continuing. "Samuel and Becky may no longer be here, but it was through their hard work and sacrifice that we still have a place to gather together in these moments. I know the hurt we experienced with Becky's passing just last month is still very fresh, but I want you all to know and believe that We. Are. Going. To. Be. Okay," he spoke with determination.

Everyone raised their drinks in agreement and sipped as Luke took his seat.

"Um, I have something to share." Jamie shuffled to his feet, and all eyes turned to him. "Cora, would you mind standing for me?"

A broad grin split Jules's face. She was sure she knew what was coming.

Cora slowly rose to her feet, looking like a deer caught in headlights as she looked around the table at the other expectant faces.

"From the first day I saw you, I was captivated by your beauty, and as I got to know you better, I was captivated by your strength, your fierce loyalty, and your love. Cora, I never thought I would ever love again, but you have won my heart like no one else."

Jamie reached into his pocket and took out a black box.

Looking from it to her, he said, "I've been carrying this with me for a while now, waiting and looking for the perfect opportunity to ask. I believe today is that day." Jamie grinned as he got down on one knee. There were collective oohs and ahhs from those around the table.

"Cora Hamilton, will you make me the happiest man alive and marry me?"

Cora's hand flew to her mouth as she stared at the round-cut diamond ring shining up at her. Tears pooled in her eyes. After what felt like a lifetime, she nodded before vocalizing her answer. "Yes, I will marry you," she said, beaming from ear to ear.

Jamie smiled triumphantly before slipping the ring onto her finger. Loud cheers erupted as he stood to his feet and kissed Cora.

Jules looked over at Erin and smirked. She looked down the table to see her father with regret written on his face. She felt a slight pang of remorse for him and quickly averted her eyes to bask in the happiness of her mother and her new fiancé. As she looked around the table at the other smiling faces, a feeling of contentment came over her.

Nine months ago, she felt as if her life was over, but today looking at her family and the man she loved sitting beside her with their daughter, she realized that was the furthest from the truth. Yes, they had been through a lot as a family, and she and Noah had faced many tests but persevered.

Uncle Luke was right. They were all going to be okay.

Coming Next in the Oak Harbor Series

You can pre order: Always & Forever

Other Books by Kimberly

The Archer Inn Series
Yuletide Creek Series
An Oak Harbor Series

Connect with Kimberly Thomas

Facebook
Newsletter
BookBub

To receive exclusive updates from Kimberly, please sign up to be on her Newsletter!

CLICK HERE TO SUBSCRIBE

Made in the USA
Monee, IL
05 March 2023